NEFERET'S CURSE

ALSO BY P. C. CAST and KRISTIN CAST

Marked

Betrayed

Chosen

Untamed

Hunted

Tempted

Burned

Awakened

Destined

Hidden

The Fledgling Handbook 101

Dragon's Oath

Lenobia's Vow

NEFERET'S CURSE

P. C. CAST and KRISTIN CAST

WITHDRAWN

ST. MARTIN'S GRIFFIN
NEW YORK

This is a work of fiction. All of the characters, organizations, and events portrayed in this novel are either products of the authors' imaginations or are used fictitiously.

www.stmartins.com

ISBN 978-1-250-00025-5 (hardcover)
ISBN 978-1-4668-0190-5 (e-book)

First Edition: February 2013

10 9 8 7 6 5 4 3 2 1

ACKNOWLEDGMENTS

Thank you to my wonderful, talented friend and illustrator, Kim Doner. Because of the tight schedule on this book she had to get in my (crazy) mind and work from my (usually erratic) brainstorming/outline ideas. Not only did she do an amazing job, but from our illustration meetings came some of the best ideas that I incorporated into Emily's story. Kim, I adore you!

To my SMP family, and especially the haggard production and design team. I owe you guys a case of champagne. And I mean good champagne.

Thank you to my friend, Robin Green Tilly, who helped me with the postscript to this novella.

As always I thank my agent and friend, Meredith Bernstein, without whom the House of Night wouldn't exist.

NEFERET'S
CURSE

January 15th, 1893
Emily Wheiler's Journal
Entry: the first

This is not a diary. I loathe the very thought of compiling my thoughts and actions in a locked book, secreted away as if they were precious jewels.

I know my thoughts are not precious jewels.

I have begun to suspect my thoughts are quite mad.

That is why I feel compelled to record them. It could be that in the re-reading, sometime in the future, I will discover why these horrible things have befallen me.

Or, I will discover that I have, indeed, lost my mind.

If that be the case, then this will serve as a record of the onset of my paranoia and madness so as to lay the foundation to discover a cure.

Do I want to be cured?

Perhaps that is a question that would be best set aside for now.

First, let me begin when everything changed. It was not on this, the first date of my journal. It was two and one half months ago, on the first day of November, in the year eighteen ninety-two. That was the morning my mother died.

Even here in the silent pages of this journal I hesitate to recall that terrible morning. My mother died in a tide of blood, which surged from within her following the birth of the small, lifeless body of my brother, Barrett, named after Father. It seemed to me then, as it does today, that Mother simply gave up when she saw that Barrett would not draw breath. It was as if even the life force that sustained her could not bear the loss of her precious only son.

Or was the full truth that she could not bear to face Father after the loss of *his* precious, only son?

That question would not have entered my mind before that morning. Until the morning my mother died, the questions that most often entered my mind were focused on how I might persuade Mother to allow me to purchase another one of the new cycling costumes that were all the rage, or how I could make my hair look exactly like a Gibson girl.

If I had thought of Father before the morning Mother died, it was as most of my girlfriends thought of their fathers—as a distant and somewhat intimidating patriarch. In my particular case, Father only praised me through Mother's comments. Actually, before Mother's death, he seemed to rarely notice me at all.

Father was not in the room when Mother died. The doctor had proclaimed the birthing process too vulgar for a man to witness, especially not a man of the import of Barrett H. Wheiler, president of the First National Bank of Chicago.

And me? Barrett and Alice Wheiler's daughter? The doctor did not mention the vulgarity of childbirth to me. Actually, the doctor did not even notice me until after Mother was dead and Father had brought me to his attention.

"Emily, you will not leave me. You will wait with me until the doctor arrives and then remain there, in the window seat. You should know what it is to be a wife and mother. You should not go blindly into it as did I." Mother had commanded me in that soft voice of hers, which made everyone who did not truly know her believe she was softheaded and no more than a beautiful, compliant bobble on Father's arm.

"Yes, Mother," I had said with a nod, and done as she had ordered.

I remember sitting, still as shadow, in the unlit window seat across from the bed in Mother's opulent bedchamber. I saw everything. It did not take her long to die.

There was so much blood. Barrett had been born in blood—a small, still, gore-covered creature. He had looked like a grotesque broken doll. After the spasm that had expelled him from between Mother's legs, the blood did not stop. It kept surging and surging while my mother wept tears as silent as her son. I knew she wept because she had turned her head away from the sight of the doctor wrapping the dead baby in linens. Mother's gaze met mine then.

I could not remain in the window seat. I rushed to the side of her bed and, while the doctor and his nurse futilely attempted to staunch the scarlet river that gushed from her, I gripped her hand and brushed the damp hair back from her forehead. Through my tears and my fear, I tried to murmur reassurance to her, and tell her that everything would be well once she rested.

Mother had squeezed my hand and whispered, "I am glad you are here with me at the end."

"No! You'll get better, Mother!" I'd protested.

"Sssh," she'd soothed. "Just hold my hand." Her voice had faded away then, but Mother's emerald eyes, which everyone said were so like mine, did not look away from me all the while her flushed face went shockingly white and her breath softened, caught, and then on a sigh, ceased altogether.

I'd kissed her hand then, and staggered back to my window seat, where I'd wept, unnoticed as the nurse performed the daunting job of disposing of the soaked linens and making Mother presentable for Father's viewing. But Father hadn't waited until Mother had been prepared for him. He'd pushed into the room, ignoring the protestations of the doctor.

"It is a son, you say?" Father had not so much as glanced at the bed. Instead he had hurried to the bassinette, wherein lay the shrouded body of Barrett.

"It *was*, indeed, a boy child," the doctor said somberly. "Born too soon, as I told you, sir. There was nothing to be done. His lungs were too weak. He never drew breath. He did not utter one cry."

"Dead . . . silent." Father had wiped a hand wearily across his face. "Do you know when Emily was born she cried so lustily I heard her in the drawing room downstairs and believed her to be a son?"

"Well, Mr. Wheiler, I know it is of little consolation after losing a son and a wife, but you do have a daughter, and through her the promise of heirs."

"*She* promised me heirs!" Father shouted, finally turning to look at Mother.

I must have made some small, wounded sound because Father's eyes instantly flicked to my window seat. They narrowed, and for a moment it didn't seem he recognized me. And then he shook himself, as if trying to shiver something uncomfortable from his skin.

"Emily, why are you here?" Father's voice had sounded so angry that it seemed the question he'd meant to ask was much more than why I was in that room at that particular time.

"M-mother bade me s-stay," I had stuttered.

"Your mother is dead," he'd said, anger flattened to hard-edged truth.

"And this is no place for a young lady." The doctor's face had been flushed when he faced my father. "Beg pardon, Mr. Wheiler. I was too occupied with the birth to notice the girl there."

"The fault was not yours, Doctor Fisher. My wife often did and said things that perplexed me. This is simply the last of them." Father made a dismissive gesture that took in the doctor, the maids, and me. "Now leave me with Mrs. Wheiler, all of you."

I wanted to run from the room—to escape as quickly as possible, but my feet had gone numb and cold from sitting unmoving for so long and as I passed Father I'd stumbled. His hand caught me under the elbow. I'd looked up, startled.

His expression had suddenly appeared to soften as he gazed down at me. "You have your mother's eyes."

"Yes." Breathless and lightheaded, that was all I could say.

"That is as it should be. You are now the Lady of Wheiler House." Then Father released me and walked slowly, heavily, to the bloody bed.

As I closed the door behind me, I heard him begin to weep.

Thereby also began my strange and lonely time of mourning. I moved numbly through the funeral and collapsed afterward. It was as if sleep had taken me over. I could not break free of it. For two full months I hardly left my bed. I did not care that I grew thin and pale. I did not care that the social condolence calls of my mother's friends and their daughters were left unanswered. I did not notice that Christmas and a New Year came and went. Mary, my mother's lady's maid, whom I had inherited, begged, cajoled, and scolded. I cared not at all.

It was the fifth day of January when Father broke me free of sleep's hold. My room had grown cold, so cold that my shivering had awakened me. The fire in my hearth had died and not been relit, so I pulled the sash attached to Mary's summoning bell, which tinkled all the way down in the servants' quarters in the bowels of the house, but she had not answered my call. I remember putting on my dressing gown, and thinking—briefly—how large it seemed and how very much it engulfed me. Making my way slowly from my third-floor bedchamber down the wide, wooden stairway, shivering, I searched for Mary. Father had emerged from his study as I came to the bottom of the stairs. When he first saw me his eyes were blank, then his expression registered surprise. Surprise followed by something I was almost certain was disgust.

"Emily, you look wretched! Thin and pale! Are you ill?"

Before I could answer, Mary was there, hurrying across the foyer toward us. "I told ye, Mr. Wheiler. She's not been eating. I said she was doing nothin' but sleepin'. Wastin' away, she is." Mary had spoken briskly, her soft Irish accent more pronounced than usual.

"Well, this behavior must end at once," Father had said sternly. "Emily, you will leave your bed. You will eat. You will take daily walks in the gardens. I simply will not have you looking emaciated. You are, after all, the Lady of Wheiler House, and my lady cannot look as if she were a starving gutter waif."

His eyes had been hard. His anger had been intimidating, especially as I realized Mother wouldn't appear from her parlor, buzzing with distracting energy and shooing me away while pacifying Father with a smile and a touch.

I took an automatic step away from him, which only made his expression darker. "You have your mother's look, but not her spunk. As irritating as it had been at times, I admired her spunk. I miss it."

"I-I miss Mother, too," I heard myself blurt.

"Of course ye do, dove," Mary had soothed. "'Tis only been little over two months."

"Then we have something in common after all." Father had ignored Mary completely and spoken as if she hadn't been there, nervously touching my hair, smoothing my dressing gown. "The loss of Alice Wheiler has created our commonality." He'd turned his head then, studying me. "You do have her look." Father stroked his dark beard and his gaze lost its hard, intimidating cast. "We shall have to make the best of her absence, you know."

"Yes, Father." I'd felt relieved at the gentling of his voice.

"Good. Then I expect you to join me for dinner each evening, as you and your mother used to. No more of this hiding in your room, starving your looks away."

I had smiled then, actually smiled. "I would like that," I'd said.

He'd grunted, slapped the newspaper he'd been holding across his arm, and nodded. "At dinner then," he'd said, and he walked past me, disappearing into the west wing of the house.

"I may be even a little hungry tonight," I'd said to Mary as she clucked at me and helped me up the stairway.

"'Tis good to see he's takin' an interest in ye, it is," Mary had whispered happily.

I'd hardly paid any attention to her. My only thought was that for the first time in a month I had something more than sleep and sadness to look forward to. Father and I shared a commonality!

I'd dressed carefully for dinner that evening, understanding for the first time how very thin I had become when my black mourning dress had to be pinned so that it did not hang unattractively loose. Mary combed my hair, twining it in a thick chignon that I thought made my newly thin face look much older than my fifteen years.

I will never forget the start it gave me when I entered our dining room and saw the two place settings—Father's, where he had always been at the head of the table—and mine, now placed at Mother's spot to Father's right hand.

He'd stood and held Mother's chair for me. I was sure as I sat that I could still smell her perfume—rose water, with just a hint of the lemon rinse she used on her hair to bring out the richness of her auburn highlights.

George, a Negro man who served our dinner, began ladling from the soup tureen. I'd worried that the silence would be terrible, but as Father began to eat, so, too, began his familiar words.

"The Columbian Exposition Committee has joined collectively behind Burnham; we are supporting him completely. I wondered, at first, that the man might be a touch mad—that he was attempting something unattainable, but his vision of Chicago's World's Columbian Exposition outshining Paris's splendor seems to be within reach, or at least his design appears to be sound—extravagant, but sound." He'd paused to take a healthy mouthful of the steak and potatoes that had replaced his empty soup bowl, and in that pause I could hear my mother's voice.

"Is not extravagance what everyone is calling for?" and didn't realize until Father looked up at me that it had been I who had spoken and not, after all, the ghost of Mother. I froze under his sharp, dark-eyed scrutiny, wishing I'd kept silent and daydreamed the meal away as I had so many times in the past.

"And how do you know what *everyone* is calling for?" His keen, dark eyes were sharp on me, but his lips lifted slightly at the corners, just as he used to almost smile at Mother.

I remember feeling a rush of relief and smiling heartily in return. His question was one I'd heard him ask Mother more times than I could begin to count. I let her words reply for me. "I know you believe all women do is talk, but they listen, too." I spoke more quickly and more softly than Mother, but Father's eyes had crinkled in the corners as he showed his approval and amusement.

"Indeed . . ." he'd said with a chuckle, cutting a large piece of bloody red meat and eating it as if he were ravenous while he gulped down glasses of wine as red and dark as the liquid that ran from his meat. "But I must keep close tabs on Burnham, and his gaggle of architects, close tabs indeed. They are grotesquely over budget, and those workmen . . . always a problem . . . always a problem . . ." Father spoke as he chewed, dribbling bits of food and wine into his beard, a habit I knew Mother had loathed, and often rebuked him for.

I did not rebuke him, nor did I loathe his well-engrained habit. I simply forced myself to eat and to make the proper noises of appreciation as he spoke on and on about the importance of fiscal responsibility and the worry that the frail health of one of the lead architects was causing the board in general. After all, Mr. Root had already succumbed to pneumonia. Some said he'd been the driving force behind the entire project, and not Burnham at all.

The dinner sped quickly by until Father had finally eaten and spoken his fill. Then he had stood, and, as I had heard him wish uncountable times to my mother, he'd said, "I shall retire to my library for a cigar and a whiskey. Have a pleasant evening, my dear, and I shall see you again, soon." I remember vividly feeling a great warmth for him as I thought, *He is treating me as if I were a woman grown—a true lady of the house!*

"Emily," he'd continued, even though he'd been rather wobbly and obviously well into his cups, "let us decide that as we have just begun a new year, it will mark a new beginning for the both of us. Shall we try to move forward together, my dear?"

Tears had come to my eyes, and I'd smiled tremulously up at him. "Yes, Father. I would like that very much."

Then, quite unexpectedly, he had lifted my thin hand in his large one, bent over it, and kissed it—just exactly as he used to kiss Mother's hand in parting. Even though his lips and beard were moist from the wine and the food, I was still smiling and feeling ever so much like a lady when, holding my hand in his, he met my gaze.

That was the first time I saw it, what I have come to think of as *the burning look*. It was as if his eyes stared so violently into mine that I feared they would cause me to combust.

"Your eyes are your mother's," he said. His words slurred and I smelled the sharp reek of his breath, heavily tainted by wine.

I found I could not speak. I only shivered and nodded.

Father dropped my hand then and walked unsteadily from the room. Before George began to clear the table, I took my linen napkin and rubbed it across the back of my hand, wiping away the wetness left there and wondering why I felt such an uneasy sensation deep in my stomach.

Madeleine Elcott and her daughter, Camille, were the first of the social calls I received two days later. Mr. Elcott was on the board at Father's bank, and Mrs. Elcott had been a great friend of Mother's, though I'd never truly understood why. Mother had been beautiful and charming, and a renowned hostess. In comparison, Mrs. Elcott had seemed waspish, gossipy, and miserly. When she and Mother sat together at dinner parties, I used to think Mrs. Elcott looked like a clucking chicken next to a dove, but she had the ability to make Mother laugh, and Mother's laughter had been so magical, it had made the reason for it unimportant. I'd once overheard Father telling Mother that she would simply have to do more entertaining because dinner parties at the Elcott mansion were short on spirits and courses, and long on talk. Had anyone ever asked for my opinion, which of course they did not, I would have agreed wholeheartedly with Father. The Elcott mansion was less than a mile from our home, and looked stately and proper from the outside, but the inside was Spartan and, actually, rather gloomy. Little wonder Camille so loved visiting me!

Camille was my best friend. She and I were close in age, she being only six months the younger. Camille talked a lot, but not in the cruel, gossipy way of her mother. Because of the closeness of our parents, Camille and I had grown up together, which had made us more like sisters than best friends.

"Oh, my poor, sad Emily! How thin and wan you look," Camille had said as she rushed into Mother's parlor and embraced me.

"Well, of course she looks thin and wan!" Mrs. Elcott had moved her daughter aside and stiffly taken my hands in hers before she'd even shed her white leather gloves. Remembering her touch, I realize now that she'd felt cold and quite reptilian. "Emily has lost her mother, Camille. Think of how wretched your life would be had you lost me. I would expect you to look just as terrible as poor Emily. I'm sure dear Alice is looking down on her daughter in understanding and appreciation."

Not expecting her to speak so freely of Mother's death, I felt a little shock at Mrs. Elcott's words. I tried to catch Camille's gaze as we moved apart, settling ourselves on the divan and matching chairs. I'd wanted to share with her our old look, one that said we agreed how sometimes our mothers could say terribly embarrassing things, but Camille seemed to be looking everywhere but at me.

"Yes, Mother, of course. I apologize," was all she muttered contritely.

Trying to feel my way through this new social world that suddenly was very foreign, I breathed a long breath of relief when the housemaid bustled in with tea and cakes. I poured. Mrs. Elcott and Camille studied me.

"You really are quite thin," Camille said finally.

"I will be better soon," I'd said, sending her a reassuring smile. "At first I found it difficult to do anything except sleep, but Father has insisted that I get well. He reminded me that I am now the Lady of Wheiler House."

Camille's gaze had flicked quickly to her mother's. I could not read the hard look in Mrs. Elcott's eyes, but it was enough to silence her daughter.

"That is quite brave of you, Emily," Mrs. Elcott spoke into the silence. "I am sure you are a great comfort to your father."

"We tried to see you for two whole months, but you wouldn't receive us, not even during the holidays. It was like you'd disappeared!" Camille blurted as I poured her tea. "I thought you'd died, too."

"I'm sorry." At first, her words had made me contrite. "I didn't mean to upset you."

"Of course you didn't," Mrs. Elcott had said, frowning at her daughter. "Camille, Emily wasn't disappearing—she was mourning."

"I still am," I'd said softly. Camille heard me and nodded, wiping her eyes, but her mother had been too busy helping herself to the iced cakes to pay either of us much attention.

There was a silence that seemed very long while we sipped our tea and I pushed the small, white cake around my plate, and then, in a high, excited voice, Mrs. Elcott asked, "Emily, were you really there? In the room with her when Alice died?"

I'd looked to Camille, wishing for an instant that she could silence her mother, but of course that had been a foolish, futile wish. My friend's face had mirrored my own discomfort, though she did not appear shocked at her mother's disregard for propriety and privacy. I realized then that Camille had known her mother was going to question me thus. I drew a deep, fortifying breath and answered truthfully, though hesitantly, "Yes. I was there."

"It must have been quite ghastly," Camille said quickly.

"Yes," I said. I'd placed my teacup carefully in its saucer before either of them could see that my hand trembled.

"I expect there had been a lot of blood," Mrs. Elcott said, nodding slowly as if in pre-agreement with my response.

"There was." I'd clasped my hands tightly together in my lap.

"When we heard you were in the room when she died, we were all so very sorry for you," Camille had said softly, hesitantly.

Shocked silent, I could almost hear Mother's voice saying sharply, *Servants and their gossip!* I was mortified that Mother's death had been the topic of gossip, but I'd also longed to talk to Camille, to tell her how frightened I'd been. But before I could collect myself enough to speak, her mother's sharp voice had intruded.

"Indeed, it was all anyone could talk about for weeks and weeks. Your poor mother would have been appalled. Bad enough that you missed the Christmas Ball, but for the topic of conversation during the evening to have been your witnessing her gruesome death . . ." Mrs. Elcott shuddered. "Alice would have thought it as dreadful as it was."

My cheeks had flamed hot. I had utterly forgotten about the Christmas Ball, and my sixteenth birthday. Both had taken place in December, when sleep had been cloaking me from life.

"Everyone was talking about me at the ball?" I'd wanted to run back to my room and never emerge.

Camille's words came fast, and she had made a vague movement, as if she understood how difficult the conversation had become for me and was trying to brush away the subject. "Nancy, Evelyn, and Elizabeth were worried about you. We were *all* worried about you—we still are."

"You left out one person who seemed especially concerned: Arthur Simpton. Remember how you said he could talk of nothing except how horrible it all must have been for Emily, even while he was waltzing with you." Mrs. Elcott hadn't sounded worried at all. She'd sounded angry.

I'd blinked and felt as if I was swimming up through deep, murky waters. "Arthur Simpton? He was talking about me?"

"Yes, while he danced with *Camille*." Mrs. Elcott's tone had been hard with annoyance, and I'd suddenly understood why—Arthur Simpton was the eldest son of a wealthy railroad family that had recently relocated from New York City to Chicago, because of close business ties with Mr. Pullman. Besides being rich, suitably bred, and eligible, he was also extremely handsome. Camille and I had whispered about him as his family moved into their South Prairie Avenue mansion and we'd watched him riding his bicycle up and down the street. Arthur had been the single driving force behind our desire to obtain our own bicycles and to join the Hermes Bicycle Club. He had also been one of the key reasons both of our mothers had agreed to pressure our fathers into allowing us to do so, even though Camille had told me she'd heard her father informing her mother that bicycle bloomers could lead a young woman into "a life of pernicious lasciviousness." I remembered it clearly because Camille had made me giggle as she'd done an excellent impression of her father. As I'd laughed she'd also said she'd be willing to enter a life of pernicious lasciviousness if it meant entering it with Arthur Simpton.

I hadn't said anything then. It hadn't seemed necessary. Arthur had, quite often, looked our way, but the both of us knew it was my eyes he met when he tipped his hat, and my name he called a "Bright, good morning, Miss Emily" to.

I shook my head, feeling woozy and slow. I turned to Camille. "Arthur Simpton? He danced with you?"

"Most of the evening," Mrs. Elcott had spoken for her daughter, nodding her head so quickly the feathers on her hat fluttered with disturbing violence, making her look even more henlike. "In truth Camille and I believe Arthur Simpton will approach Mr. Elcott soon and ask permission to formally court her."

My stomach had felt terrible and hollow. How could he court Camille? Little over two months ago he hadn't so much as spoken her name to wish her a good morning. Could such a short amount of time change him so drastically?

Yes, I'd decided silently and quickly. Yes, a short amount of time could change anyone drastically. It had certainly changed me.

I'd opened my mouth to speak, though I was still not sure what it was I was going to say, and Father had burst into the room, looking frazzled and wearing no jacket.

"Ah, Emily, here you are." He'd nodded absently to Mrs. Elcott and Camille, saying, "Good afternoon, ladies." Then he'd turned his full attention to me. "Emily, which waistcoat should I wear this evening? The black or the burgundy? The board is meeting again with those infernal architects, and I need to use a firm hand. The right tone must be set. Their budget is out of control and time is short. The fair must open May the first. They are simply not prepared. They climb too steep—too steep!"

I blinked, trying to focus on the bizarre scene. Arthur Simpton's name linked with Camille's had still been almost tangible in the air around us while Father stood there, his dress shirt untucked and only partially buttoned, a waistcoat in each hand, waving them about as if they were flags unfurled. Mrs. Elcott and Camille were staring at him as if he had lost his mind.

I was suddenly angry, and I'd automatically come to Father's defense.

"Mother always said the black is more formal, but the burgundy is richer. Wear the burgundy, Father. The architects should see you as rich enough to control the money and, therefore, their futures." I'd tried my best to pitch my voice softly to mimic my mother's soothing tone.

Father had nodded. "Yes, yes, it should be as your mother said. The richer is the better. Yes, well done." He'd bowed briskly to the other two women, wishing them a good day, and then he hurried out. Before the door closed, I could see his valet, Carson, joining him in the hallway and taking the discarded black waistcoat that was tossed his way.

When I turned back to the Elcott women, I lifted my chin. "As you can see, Father has been depending upon me."

Mrs. Elcott had lifted a brow and sniffed. "I do see. Your father is a fortunate man, and the man to whom he eventually marries you will be fortunate, as well, to have such a well-trained wife." Her gaze went to her daughter and then she smiled silkily as she'd continued, "Though I imagine your father won't want to part with you for several years, so marriage is out of the question for your foreseeable future."

"Marriage?" A jolt had gone through me at the word. Camille and I had talked about it, of course, but we had mostly whispered about the courting, the betrothal, the sumptuous wedding . . . and not the actual marriage itself. Mother's voice had suddenly echoed from my memory: *Emily, you will not leave me . . . You should know what it is to be a wife and mother. You should not go blindly into it as did I.* I'd felt a shudder of panic and added, "Oh, I couldn't possibly think about marriage now!"

"Of course you can't think about marriage right now! Neither of us should—not really. We're sixteen. That's entirely too young. Isn't that what you've always said, Mother?" Camille had sounded strained, almost frightened.

"Thinking about a thing and preparing for a thing are not one and the same, Camille. Opportunity should not be overlooked. And *that* is what I have always said." Mrs. Elcott had peered down her long nose at me while she spoke with disdain.

"Well, I think it is a good thing that I am devoted to my father," I'd responded, feeling horribly uncomfortable and unsure of what else to say.

"Oh, we are all in agreement about that!" Mrs. Elcott had said.

They hadn't stayed long after Father's appearance. Mrs. Elcott had rushed Camille off, not giving us even one small chance to speak to each other alone. It was as if she'd gotten what she'd come for and left satisfied.

And me? What had I gotten?

I'd hoped for validation. Even though the affection of the handsome young Arthur Simpton had turned from me to my friend, I'd believed it was my duty as a daughter to care for my father. I'd felt that Camille and her mother would see that I was doing my best to carry on after Mother—that in a little over two months I'd grown from girl to woman. I'd thought that somehow I could make the loss of Mother bearable.

But in the long, silent hours after their visit, my mind had begun to replay the events and to view their facets differently, and on retrospection I feel my second view to be more valid than my first. Mrs. Elcott had wanted substantiation of the gossip; she'd gotten her wish. She had also wanted to make it very clear that Arthur Simpton would not now be a part of my future and that no man—other than Father—would be a part of my foreseeable future. She had accomplished both tasks.

I'd sat up that night and waited for Father's return. Even now, as I record what happened next, I cannot fault myself for my actions. As the Lady of Wheiler Mansion, it was my duty to see Father cared for—to be there with a tea or possibly a brandy for him—as I'd imagined Mother had often done upon his late return from work dinners. I had expected Father to be tired. I had expected him to be himself: aloof, gruff, and overbearing, yet polite and appreciative of my fidelity.

I had not expected him to be drunk.

I'd seen Father filled with wine. I had glimpsed him red nosed and effusive in his praise of Mother's beauty as they went out in the evenings, dressed formally and trailing the scent of lavender, lemon, and cabernet. I cannot remember ever seeing them upon their return. Had I not been asleep in my bed, I would have been brushing my hair or embroidering the fine details of violets at the bodice of my newest day dress.

I realize now that Father and Mother had been to me like distant moons circling the self-absorption of my youth.

That night Father evolved from moon to burning sun.

He'd lurched inside the foyer, calling loudly for his valet, Carson. I'd been in Mother's parlor, trying to keep my heavy eyes open by rereading Emily Brontë's gothic novel, *Wuthering Heights*. At the sound of his voice, I'd put the book aside and hurried to him. His scent came to me before I saw him. I remember that I pressed a hand against my nose, flustered at the rankness of brandy, sweat, and cigars. As I write this, I am afraid that those three odors will for me, forever, be the scent of man, and the scent of nightmares.

I'd rushed to his side, pursing my lips at the thick reek of his breath, thinking that he must not be well.

"Father, are you ill? Shall I call the physician?"

"Physician? No, no, no! Right as rain. I'm right as rain. Just need some help getting to Alice's room. Not as young as I used to be—not at all. But I can still do my duty. I'll get her with a son yet!" Father swayed as he talked, and he'd put a heavy hand on my shoulder to steady himself.

I staggered under his weight, guiding him to the wide stairway, so worried that he was ill that I hardly comprehended what he was saying. "I'm here. I'll help you," was what I whispered over and over to him. He'd leaned even more heavily on me as we climbed clumsily up to the second floor and finally stopped outside his bedchamber. He'd shaken his head back and forth, mumbling, "This isn't her room."

"It is your bedchamber," I'd said, wishing his valet or *anyone* would appear.

He'd squinted at me, as if he were having trouble focusing. Then his slack, drunken expression had changed. "Alice? So, you *are* willing to break your frigid rules and join my bed tonight."

His hand had been hot and damp on the shoulder of my fine linen nightgown.

"Father, it's me, Emily."

"Father?" He'd blinked and brought his face down closer to mine. His breath had almost made me retch. "Emily. Indeed. It is you. Yes, you. I know you now. You cannot be Alice, she is dead." His face still so very close to mine, he added, "You're too thin, but you do have her eyes." He'd reached out then and lifted a strand of the thick, auburn hair that had escaped my nightcap. "And her hair. You have her hair." He'd rubbed my hair between his fingers and slurred, "You must eat more—shouldn't be so thin." Then, bellowing for Carson to attend him, Father let loose my hair, shoved me aside, and staggered into his room.

I should have retreated to my own bed then, but a terrible unease had come over me and I ran, allowing my feet to carry me where they willed. When I finally halted, gasping to catch my breath, I found my blind flight had taken me into the gardens that stretched for more than five acres in the rear of our house. There I collapsed on a stone bench that sat, concealed, under the curtain of a massive willow tree, and put my face in my hands and wept.

Then something magical happened. The warm night breeze lifted the willow branches and the clouds blew away, exposing the moon. Though only a slim crescent, it was almost silver in its brilliance, and it seemed to beam metallic light into the garden, setting aglow the huge white marble fountain that was its central feature. Within the fountain, spewing water from his open mouth, was the Greek god Zeus, in the form of the bull that had tricked and then abducted the maiden, Europa. The fountain had been a wedding gift from Father to Mother, and had been at the heart of Mother's extensive garden since my earliest memories.

Perhaps it was because the fountain was Mother's, or perhaps it was from envy for the musicality of the bubbling water, but my tears stopped as I studied it. Eventually, my heartbeat slowed and my breathing became normal. And, even when the moon became cloaked by clouds once again, I remained beneath the tree, listening to the water and allowing it, as well as the concealing willow shadows, to soothe me until I knew I could sleep. Then I slowly made my way up to my third-floor bedchamber. That night I dreamed I was Europa and the white bull was carrying me away to a beautiful meadow where no one ever died and where I was, eternally, young and carefree.

April 15th, 1893
Emily Wheiter's Journal

I should have written in my journal before now, but the months since my last entry have been so confusing—so difficult—that I have not been myself. Childishly, I thought that by not writing, not recording the events that have unfolded, I could make it seem as if they had not happened—would not continue to happen.

I was so very wrong.

Everything has changed, and I must use this journal as evidence. Even if I am losing my mind, it will show an unraveling of madness and, as I originally hoped, provide a path for my treatment. And if, as I am coming to suspect, I am not mad, a record of these events should be made and might, somehow, aid me if I must choose a new future.

Let me begin anew.

After that cold night in January when Father returned home drunk, I have never waited up for him again. I tried not to think much on it—tried not to remember his breath, the hot, heavy feel of his hand, and the things he'd said.

Instead, when he departed for late dinner meetings, I wished him a pleasant good evening, and said I would be sure Carson attended to him when he returned.

At first that stopped his burning looks. I was so busy with the running of Wheiler House that except for our dinners together, I saw Father very little.

But over the past months the dinners had changed. Rather, the dinners hadn't changed—the amount of wine consumed by Father is what changed. The more Father drank, the more often his eyes burned into me as he bid me good night.

I began to carefully water his wine. He has not, yet, noticed.

And then I threw all of my attention into taking complete responsibility for the running of Wheiler House. Yes, of course, Mary and Carson helped me . . . advised me. The cook made grocer lists, but I approved the menus. As Mary had once commented, it was as if my mother's spirit had taken me over, and I was a girl no more.

I tried to tell myself that was a good thing—a lovely compliment. The truth was then as it is today—I think I did my duty, and continue to do my duty—but I am not sure that is a good thing at all.

It is not simply the work of being Lady of Wheiler House that has so changed me. It is how people began to change in their treatment of me. Yes, at first I had been overwhelmed by the extent of Mother's duties. I'd had no idea that she not only ran the household, instructed the servants, saw to every detail of Father's routine, supervised me, *and* volunteered twice a week at the General Federation of Women's Club, helping to feed and care for the homeless women and children of Chicago. Mother had been dead five months, and during that time I had completely dedicated myself to being Lady of Wheiler House. Thus when Evelyn Field and Camille called on me one midmorning early last month, asking if I would like to join them in riding our bicycles to the shore and picnicking, I'd been justifiably overwhelmed with the joy the freedom of the moment provided, especially as I had thought that Father had already left for the bank.

"Oh, yes!" I'd said happily, putting down my fountain pen and pushing aside the grocer list I'd been going over. I remember how happy Evelyn and Camille had been when I'd said yes. The three of us had laughed spontaneously.

"Emily, I am so, so glad you will come with us." Camille had hugged me. "And you are looking so well—not pale and thin at all."

"No, not pale at all!" Evelyn agreed. "You're as beautiful as ever."

"Thank you, Evelyn. I have missed everyone so much." I'd hesitated, feeling the need to share a confidence with someone who wasn't a servant—or my father. "It has been difficult since Mother has been gone. Really difficult." Camille had chewed her lip. Evelyn had looked as if she were on the verge of tears. I quickly wiped my cheeks with the back of my hand, and found my smile again. "But now that the both of you are here I'm feeling much lighter than I have for weeks and weeks."

"That's what we intended. Mother tried to tell me you were too busy to be bothered with bicycle riding, but I swore not to listen to her and called on you anyway," Camille had said.

"Your mother is always too serious," Evelyn said, rolling her eyes skyward. "We all know that."

"I don't believe she was *ever* young," Camille had said, making us giggle.

I was still giggling as I hurried from the parlor, determined to rush up the stairs and change as quickly as possible into my riding bloomers when I'd run straight into Father.

The breath had been knocked out of me with an *oof*, and my eyes had teared.

"Emily, why ever would you be bolting from the parlor in such an uncivilized manner?" Father had seemed a storm cloud in the making.

"E-excuse me, Father," I'd stuttered. "Camille Elcott and Evelyn Field have called on me and asked that I bike to the lake with them for luncheon. I was hurrying to change my clothes."

"Bicycling is excellent for the heart. It creates a strong constitution, though I do not approve of young people biking together with no adult supervision."

I hadn't noticed the tall woman standing across the foyer from Father until she'd spoken. She'd taken me by surprise, and I'd stood there, speechless, staring at her. In her deep blue dress and her peacock-plumed hat, she'd made quite an imposing figure, though one I had not recognized, and I'd wanted to say that I did not approve of old women wearing wildly plumed hats, but of course I'd held my tongue.

"Emily, do you not remember Mrs. Armour? She is chairwoman of the General Federation of Women's Club," Father had prompted me.

"Oh, yes. Mrs. Armour, I apologize for not recognizing you." I had recognized her name, now that Father had spoken it, but I could not remember the woman herself. "And—and I also apologize for rushing out," I'd continued hastily. "I do not mean to be impolite"— I'd turned and made a gesture that took in Evelyn and Camille where they sat in the parlor, watching with obvious curiosity—"but as you can see, my friends are waiting for me. Father, I will ring for Mary to bring tea if you are entertaining Mrs. Armour in your study."

"You mistake me, Miss Wheiler. It is you, and not your father with whom I wish to visit."

I'd been confused, and I believe I gaped rather stupidly at the old woman.

Father had not been likewise confused. "Emily, Mrs. Armour has called on you to speak about your inherited place at the GFWC. It was a passion of your mother's. I expect it to be a passion of yours, as well."

My confusion cleared as I realized why the name Armour had been familiar. Philip Armour was one of the wealthiest men in Chicago and he kept much of his money in Father's bank. I'd turned to Mrs. Armour and made myself smile, pitching my voice to be soft and soothing, just as Mother used to sound. "I would be honored to inherit Mother's place at the GFWC. Perhaps we can set a date for me to come to Market Hall and meet with you about—"

Suddenly, Father's big hand engulfed my elbow, squeezing while he commanded, "You will meet with Mrs. Armour now, Emily." In comparison to my gentleness, Father was like a battlefield. I heard Evelyn and Camille both gasp at his forcefulness.

Then Camille was there at my side, saying, "We can easily call again, Emily. Please, your mother's work is so much more important than our silly bicycle outing."

"Yes, truly," Evelyn had added as my friends moved hastily to the door. "We'll call again."

The sound of the door closing behind them had seemed to me like the sealing of a tomb.

"Ah, well, that is better. Enough of that foolishness," Father said as he loosed my elbow.

"Mrs. Armour, please, join me in the parlor and I will ring Mary for tea," I'd said.

"Good. Go on about your business, Emily. I will see you at dinner. Good girl—good girl," Father had said gruffly. He bowed to Mrs. Armour, and then left us alone together in the foyer.

"I can tell you are a young woman of excellent character," Mrs. Armour said as I woodenly led her into Mother's parlor. "I am sure we will get on well together, just as your mother and I did."

I nodded and agreed and let the old woman talk on and on about the importance of women of means being united in their dedication to improving the community through volunteer service.

In the weeks that have followed, I have come to realize how ironic it was that Mrs. Armour, who lectured unendingly about the

importance of the unity of women, has become one of the main in-
struments in isolating me from other women my age. You see, Evelyn and Camille have not called again to ask that I bike with them.
Evelyn has not called on me at all since that morning. Camille, well,
Camille was different. It would take more to lose her as a friend,
much more.

March passed into April—the winter chill was tempered by a spring
that came with light, reviving showers. My life has aligned itself into
a numbing rhythm. I run the household. I volunteer at the wretched
Market Hall, feeding the poor while I nod and agree with the old
women who surround me when they drone on and on about how,
because the spotlight of the world would shortly be on us and the
World's Fair, we must use our every resource to change and shape
Chicago from a barbaric gathering into a modern city. I have dinner
with Father. I watch, and I have learned.

I learned not to interrupt Father. He liked to speak while we ate
dinner. Speak—not *talk*. Father and I did not talk. He spoke and I
listened. I wanted to believe that my taking Mother's place in the
household and at dinner was honoring her memory, and at the first
I did believe it. But soon I began to see that I was not doing anything at all except providing the vessel into which Father poured his

vitriolic opinion of the world. Our nightly dinners were a stage for his soliloquy of anger and disdain.

I continue to secretly water Father's wine. Sober, he was abrupt, overbearing, and boorish. Drunk, he was terrifying. He did not beat me—he has never beaten me—though I almost wish he would. At the very least that would be a sure and outward sign of his abuse. What Father does instead is burn me with his eyes. I have come to loathe his hot, penetrating gaze.

Though how can that be? And, better asked, why? Why did I come to loathe a simple look? The answer, I hope—I pray, will unravel here, in the pages of this journal.

Camille visited, though less and less often. The problem wasn't that our friendship had ended. Not at all! She and I were still as close as sisters when we were together. The problem was that we were less and less able to be together. Mrs. Armour and Father decided that I must continue Mother's work. So I ladled soup to the miserably starving and handed out clothing to the stinking homeless three days per week. That left a mere two days out of the five, when Father worked, for Camille and I to visit. And for me to escape, though it has become more and more clear to me that escape is not possible.

I tried to get away from Wheiler House and to call on Camille as

I had before Mother's death. I attempted this four times; Father thwarted me each time. The first time, leaving late for his banking duties, Father spied me as I was hurrying away astraddle my neglected bicycle. He didn't come into the street to call me back. No. He sent Carson after me. The poor, aged valet had turned red as a ripe apple as he'd jogged along South Prairie Avenue to catch up with me.

"A bicycle is not ladylike!" Father had blustered when I'd reluctantly followed Carson home.

"But Mother never minded that I rode my bicycle. She even allowed me to join the Hermes Bicycle Club with Camille and the rest of the girls!" I'd protested.

"Your mother is dead, and you are no longer one of the *rest of the girls*." Father's eyes had traveled from my gaze down my body, taking in my modest bicycle bloomers and my serviceable, unadorned flat leather shoes. "What you are wearing is lewd."

"Father, bicycle bloomers are what all the girls wear."

His eyes continued to stare at me, burning me from my waist down. I had to fist my hands at my sides to keep from covering myself.

"I can see the shape of your body—your legs." His voice sounded odd, breathless.

My stomach heaved. "I-I will not wear them again," I heard myself saying.

"Be sure you do not. It isn't proper—not proper at all." His hot gaze finally left me. He pushed his hat firmly on his head and bowed sardonically to me. "I shall see you at dinner, where you will behave as, and be dressed in the fashion of, a civilized lady, worthy of her position as mistress of my home. Do you understand me?"

"Yes, Father."

"Carson!"

"Yes, sir!" His poor valet, who had been hovering nervously in the corner of the foyer had jumped at Father's violent tone and skittered to him, reminding me of a large, old beetle.

"See that Miss Wheiler remains at home today, where she belongs. And get rid of that infernal bicycle!"

"Very good, sir. I will do as you say . . ." The old wretch had simpered and bowed as Father had stalked from the house.

Alone with him, Caron's eyes flicked from mine to the tapestry on the wall behind us, then to the chandelier, then to the floor—everywhere except truly meeting my gaze. "Please, Miss. You know I can't let you leave."

"Yes. I know." I chewed my lip and added, hesitantly, "Carson, could you, perhaps, move my bicycle from the outbuilding to the gardening shed at the rear of the grounds instead of actually getting rid of it? Father never goes there—he'll not know. I'm sure he'll be more reasonable soon, and allow me to return to my club."

"I would like to, Miss, I would. But I cannot disobey Mr. Wheiler. Ever."

I'd turned on my heels and slammed the door to the parlor that had become mine. I hadn't really been angry with Carson, nor did I blame him. I did understand all too well what it was to be Father's puppet.

That night I dressed carefully for dinner in my most modest gown. Father hardly glanced at me while he talked endlessly about the bank, the precarious state of finances in the city, and the impending World's Fair. I rarely spoke. I nodded demurely and made agreeable noises when he paused. He drank goblet after goblet of the secretly watered wine and ate an entire rack of rare lamb.

It wasn't until he stood and bade me good night that his gaze lingered on mine. I could see that, despite the weakened wine, he'd had enough of it to flush his cheeks.

"Good night, Father," I said quickly.

His gaze scalded from my eyes to my lips. I flattened them together, wishing they were less full, less pink.

The gaze then went from my lips to the high bodice of my dress. Then, quite abruptly, he met my eyes again.

"Tell Cook to have the lamb more often. And have her be sure it is as rare next time as it was tonight. I find I have a taste for it," he said.

"Yes, Father." I kept my voice soft and low. "Good night," I repeated.

"You know you have your mother's eyes."

My stomach heaved. "Yes. I know. Good night, Father," I said for the third time.

Finally, without another word, he'd left the room.

I went to my bedchamber and sat in my window seat, my neatly folded bicycling bloomers in my lap. I watched the moon rise and begin to climb its way down the sky, and when the night was at its darkest, I made my way carefully, quietly, down the stairs, and out the rear door that led to the path, which emptied into our elaborate gardens. As I'd walked past the great bull fountain, I pretended that I was just another of the shadows surrounding it—not a living thing . . . not a girl who could be discovered.

I'd found my way to the utility shed and discovered a shovel. Behind the shed, at the edge of our property, I went to the pile of rotting compost the laborers used as fertilizer. Not heeding the smell, I dug deeply, until I'd been certain they would be safely hidden—and I'd buried my bloomers.

Afterward, I returned the shovel and washed my hands in the rainwater barrel. Then I went to my stone bench beneath the willow tree. I sat within its dark, comforting curtain until my stomach stopped heaving and I was quite sure I would not be sick. Then I sat some more, allowing the shadows and the darkness of the night to soothe me.

Though not on bicycle—never again on bicycle—I made my way to Camille's home three more times, walking the short distance down South Prairie Avenue to the Elcott mansion. Two of the three times she and I had managed to stroll toward the lake, wanting to catch a glimpse of the magical world that was being created from marsh and sand, and had the whole city abuzz.

Mrs. Elcott's maid had intercepted us both times with the urgent message that I was needed at home. When I returned home there was always something to be tended to, but that something was never urgent. And each evening Father drank heavily, his hot gaze focusing on me more and more frequently.

So, you see, it was madness for me to go to Camille a third time. Isn't it madness to do a thing again and again, and expect a different outcome? Does that not make me mad?

But I do not feel mad. I feel very much myself. My mind is clear. My thoughts are my own. I miss Mother, but the numbness of mourning has left me. What has replaced it is a waiting, wondering sense of dread. To combat the dread I have come to crave the normalcy of my old life so desperately that it is beyond my ability to translate it into words.

Perhaps I am having a bout of hysterics.

But I don't lose my breath, or faint, or burst into flamboyant tears. So, is the coolness of my temperament more proof that I am mad? Or could how I feel be much like how any girl would feel whose mother's death had so untimely come? Is Father's hot gaze only a symptom of his widower's grief? I do, indeed, have my mother's eyes.

Whatever is true, I could not stay away from Camille and the life I missed so very much. This very afternoon I visited Camille again. We did not attempt to leave the Elcott home this time. It was an unspoken agreement between us that we knew our visit would end abruptly with Carson coming to escort me home. Camille embraced me and then called for tea in the old nursery that had been made over into a rose wallpapered parlor for the Elcott daughters. While we were alone Camille had grasped my hand.

"Emily, I am so very glad to see you! I've been worried! When I called on you last Wednesday, your father's valet told me you were unavailable. That is exactly what he said the Friday before as well."

"I was *unavailable*." I curled my lip and empathized the word. "Both days I was at dreary Market Hall, being a servant to the homeless of Chicago."

Camille's smooth brow furrowed. "Then you haven't been ill?"

I snorted. "Not ill of body, but ill of mind and heart. It is as if Father expects me to take Mother's place in all things."

Camille fanned herself with her delicate fingers. "I'm so relieved! I thought you might have been struck by the pneumonia. You know Evelyn died of it last week."

I felt a shudder of shock. "I didn't know. No one told me. How terrible . . . how very terrible."

"Don't be frightened. You look strong and as beautiful as ever."

I shook my head. "Beautiful and strong? I feel as if I am one thousand years old, and that the whole world has passed me by. I miss you and I miss my old life so very much!"

"Mother says what you're doing is more important than the girls' games we used to play, and I know she must be right—being lady of a great house is very important."

"But I'm *not* the Lady of a great house! I am more servant than anything else." I felt as if I wanted to explode. "I'm not allowed to breathe one bit of freedom."

Camille tried to put a cheery face on my changes. "It is the middle of April. In two weeks it will be six months since your mother's death. Then you will be free of mourning and be able to rejoin society."

"I don't know if I can even bear two more weeks of everything being so very dreary and so very *boring* until then." I'd chewed my lip at Camille's surprised look, and hurried to explain. "Being the Lady of Wheiler House is a job—a terribly serious job. Everything must be just so—and just so means exactly how Father wants it, which is how Mother had it. I didn't understand how hard and grim it is to be a wife." I drew a deep breath and said, "She tried to tell me. That day. The day she died. That is why I was in the birthing room with her. Mother said she wanted me to know what it was to be a wife, and to not go blindly into it as she had. So I watched. Camille, I watched her die in a flood of blood, with no loving husband holding her hand and mourning at her side. That is what it is to be a wife— loneliness and death. Camille, we must never get married!"

Camille had been stirring her tea quite manically while I'd been unburdening myself of thoughts I'd been longing to share with someone. She dropped her spoon at my exclamation. I'd watched her gaze flick nervously to the closed parlor-room door, and then back to me. "Emily, I do not think it is good that you linger on thoughts of your mother's death. It cannot be healthy."

I understand now, as I record our conversation, that I had begun to say more than Camille could bear to hear and I should have ended the subject and kept my thoughts to myself and to this, my silent, nonjudgmental, journal. But then all I had wanted was someone to talk with—to share my growing fears and frustrations with, so I continued. "My thoughts *must* linger on her death. Mother herself wished it so. It was she who insisted I be there. She who wanted me to know the truth. I think, maybe, Mother knew her death was near and that she was trying to warn me—trying to show me that I should choose a different path than that of wife and mother."

"A different path? Whatever can you mean? Religious work?"

Camille and I had curled our noses together, our minds completely alike in this aspect.

"Hardly! You should see the spinsters from the church who volunteer at the GFWC. They are so drawn and pathetic, like unfed sparrows pecking at the scraps of life. No, I've been thinking about the lovely little shops that have opened around the Loop. If I can run Wheiler House, certainly I can run a simple hat shop."

"Your father would never allow that!"

"If I could make my own way, I would not need his permission," I'd said firmly.

"Emily," Camille had said, sounding worried and a little frightened. "You cannot be thinking of leaving home. All sorts of terrible things happen to girls with no family and no money." She'd lowered her voice and leaned closer to me. "You know the vampyres just moved into their palace. They bought all of Grant Park for their terrible school!"

I'd shrugged dismissively. "Yes, yes, Father's bank handled the transaction. He's talked endlessly about them and their money. They call the school a House of Night. Father says it's completely walled off from the rest of the city and guarded constantly by their own warriors."

"But they drink blood! They are *vampyres*!"

I'd been thoroughly irritated that the subject of the miserable state of my life had been overshadowed by one of Father's clients. "Camille, vampyres are rich. Everyone knows that. They have schools in many American cities as well as the capitals of Europe. They even helped to finance the building of the Eiffel Tower for Paris's World's Fair."

"I heard Mother say vampyre women are in charge of their society," Camille had whispered while she glanced at the parlor door again.

"If that is true I say good for them! Were I a vampyre, I could choose not to be trapped by my father into pretending to be my mother."

Camille's eyes had widened. I'd definitely found a way to turn the conversation back to my troubles. "Emily, he couldn't want you to pretend to be your mother. That makes no sense."

"Sense or no, that is how it seems to me."

"You must look at it with different eyes, Emily. Your poor father simply needs your help through this difficult time."

I'd felt as if the inside of me was beginning to boil, and I couldn't stop my words. "I hate it, Camille. I hate trying to take Mother's place."

"Of course you would hate feeling like you must make up for your Mother's absence. I can hardly imagine all that there is for you to do," Camille had said, nodding somberly. "But when you are the great Lady of a house, there are also jewels to buy and dresses to be commissioned and brilliant parties to host." She'd found her smile again as she'd poured more tea into my cup. "As soon as you're out of mourning, all *that* will be your responsibility, too." She'd giggled and I'd stared at her, realizing she had no understanding at all of what I was trying to tell her. When I didn't speak, she went on, chattering happily, as if both of us were carefree girls. "The Columbian Exposition opens in two weeks, just in time for you to be out of mourning. Think of it! Your father will probably need you to host dinner parties for all sorts of foreign dignitaries."

"Camille, Father won't allow me to bicycle. He cuts short my visits with you. I cannot imagine him allowing me to host dinner parties for foreigners," I'd tried to explain, to make her understand.

"But that is what your mother would do, and as you have said, he has made it clear that you inherited her place in the household."

"He has made it clear that I am trapped to be his slave and his imaginary wife!" I'd shouted. "The only time for myself I can manage are the few minutes I steal with you, and the time I spend in Mother's garden—and then only at night. During the daylight hours he has the servants spy on me and sends them after me if he's displeased by where I'm going or what I'm doing. You know that! Even here they come fetch me as if I am an escaped prisoner. Being the Lady of a great house isn't a fantasy come true—it is a waking nightmare."

"Oh, Emily! I do hate seeing you so distraught. Remember what Mother said all those months ago—the care you're taking of your father will make the man who becomes your husband very happy. I envy you, Emily."

"Don't envy me." I saw that the coldness in my voice hurt her, but I could not help myself. "I have no mother, and I'm trapped with a man whose eyes burn me!" I broke off my words and pressed the back of my hand against my mouth.

I knew the instant her expression changed from concern to

shock, and then to disbelief that I had made a dire mistake in speaking the truth.

"Emily, whatever do you mean by that?"

"Nothing," I'd assured her. "I'm tired, that's all. I misspoke. And I shouldn't be taking up all our time together just talking about me. I want to hear about you! So, tell me, has Arthur Simpton made his courtship of you formal yet?"

As I knew it would, mention of Arthur took away all other thoughts from Camille's mind. Though he hadn't spoken to her father yet, Camille had, several times, ridden side by side with him during the Hermes Club's mid-morning lakeshore route. He'd even chatted with her the day before about how intrigued he was about the enormous Ferris wheel everyone could see being erected on the Midway of the exposition grounds.

I was going to tell Camille I was happy for her, and that I wished her well with Arthur, but the words wouldn't form in my mouth. It wasn't that I was being selfish or envious. It was simply that I could not stop thinking of the unalterable fact that should Arthur court Camille it would come to be one day, in the not too distance future, that my friend would find herself in servitude to him, waiting to die alone in a flood of blood . . .

"Beg pardon, Miss Elcott. Mr. Wheiler's valet is here to collect Miss Wheiler." When Camille's maid had interrupted I realized I hadn't been listening to what Camille had been saying for several minutes.

"Thank you," I said, getting up quickly. "I really must get back."

"Miss Wheiler, the valet asked that I give this note to you, and that you deliver it to Miss Elcott."

"A note? For me? How exciting!" Camille had said. With a stomach filled with dread, I passed it to her eager fingers. She'd opened it quickly, read it, blinked twice, and then a radiant smile transformed her face from pretty to beautiful. "Oh, Emily, it's from your father. Instead of your having to rush here whenever you can find time, he has invited me to call on you at Wheiler House and to visit with you in the formal parlor." She'd squeezed my hands happily. "You won't have to leave the house at all. See, it is just like you're a great Lady! I'll come straightaway next week. Perhaps Elizabeth Ryerson will join me."

"That would be nice," I'd said woodenly before following Carson to the black carriage that waited outside. When he closed the door behind me, I felt as if I couldn't catch my breath. The entire ride back to Wheiler House, I had spent gasping for air, as would a fish held out of the water.

As I finish this, my first journal entry in months, I remind myself that I must never forget Camille's response to my confidence. She reacted with shock and confusion, and then she reverted to our girlish dreams.

If I am mad, I must keep my thoughts to myself for fear no one else *can* understand them.

If I am not mad, but am truly as much a prisoner as I am coming to believe I am, I must keep my thoughts to myself for fear no one else *will* understand them.

In either scenario there is one constant—it is only upon myself I can rely and upon my own wits to devise a way to save myself, providing salvation for me exists at all.

No! I will not fall into melancholia. I live in a modern world. Young women can leave home and find new lives—different futures. I must use my wits and my wiles. I will find a way to be the conductor of my own life! I will!

Once again, I find myself recording my innermost thoughts in my journal as I await the rise of the moon and its heralding of the deepest darkness of night so that I may go to my one true escape—the shadows of the garden and the concealing comfort I find there. The night has become my security, my shield, and my comfort—let us hope that it doesn't also become my shroud . . .

April 19th, 1893
Emily Wheiler's Journal

My hands shake as I write.

I must make them stop! I must record all that has happened with accuracy. If I leave legible record of it, I shall be able to look back upon the events of the past several days when my mind is calmer, more rational, and I may then relive every bit of discovery and wonder, and not because I believe I could be mad! No, not at all! I wish to record my remembrances for a much different, a much more joyous reason. I have discovered the way to a new future! Or rather, *he* has discovered me! Someday I know I will wish to sift through the web of events that have caught me up, have carried me on a tide of surprise and joy and—*yes I will confess it here, perhaps even love!* Someday, when my own children are grown—*yes, I may indeed embrace the path of wife and mother*—I can reread this and tell them the story of my romance with their beloved father and how he saved me from bondage and fear.

My mind and my heart are filled with Arthur Simpton! So filled that even my loathing for my odious father cannot ruin my joy, for I have found my way free of my bondage to him and to Wheiler house!

But I begin too quickly! I must go back and show how the puzzle pieces fit together to create the beautiful scene that culminated this night! Oh, happy, happy, night!

The afternoon I returned from Camille's home Father awaited me in Mother's parlor. "Emily, I would have a word with you!" he'd bellowed as I'd tried to hurry up the stair to retreat to my third-floor bedchamber.

My hands trembled and I felt as if I might be sick, but I did not balk when he called me to him. I went to the parlor and stood, ramrod straight, hands fisted at my sides, my expression calm, unflinching. I knew one thing beyond all others—Father must not sense the depth of my fear and my loathing for him. He wanted a complacent daughter. I'd been newly determined to allow him to believe he possessed what he wanted. I had meant my first step to freedom to begin at that moment. Father did not want me to socialize with my old friends, and so I would capitulate, wait, and as he became more and more certain of my submissive compliance to all of his demands, his focus would turn away from me. *Then* I would plan and execute my eventual escape.

"Father, I will not see Camille again." I'd said, mimicking Mother's sweet, soft tone. "Not if it displeases you."

He'd brushed away my words with an abruptly dismissive gesture. "That girl is not of our concern. If you insist, you may see her here, as your mother took social calls here. We have issues of much greater import to discuss." He'd pointed at the divan and ordered, "Sit!" Then he'd bellowed for tea and brandy.

"Brandy at this hour?" I regretted it the moment after I'd spoken. I'd been so foolish! I must learn to always control my words, my expression, my very bearing.

"Do you dare question me?" He'd spoken only after the maid had left the room. He had not raised his voice, but the danger in his quiet anger shivered across my skin.

"No! I only question the hour. It is but three o'clock. Am I wrong, Father? I believed brandy an evening drink."

His shoulders had relaxed and he'd chuckled as he sipped from the wide-mouthed crystal glass. "Ah, I forget you are so young and that you have so much to learn. Emily, brandy is a man's drink, one that true men take when they so will. You should begin to understand that women must behave a certain way, a way in which society dictates. That is because you are the weaker sex, and must be protected by tradition and by those who are wiser, more worldly. As for myself? I am a man who will never be a slave to social convention." He'd taken another long drink from the glass, and refilled it as he continued. "And that brings me to my point. Social convention dictates we spend at least six months in mourning for your mother, and we have practically fulfilled that time. Should anyone question us, well, I say in the face of the World's Columbian Exposition that social convention be damned!"

I'd stared at him, uncomprehending.

Father had laughed aloud. "You look exactly as your mother did after the first time I kissed her. That was the first night we'd met. I'd gone against social convention then, too!"

"I'm sorry, Father. I do not understand."

"As of today I am lifting our mourning period." When I gaped silently he waved his hand, as if wiping away soot from a window.

"Oh, some will be shocked, but most will understand that the opening of the World's Columbian Exposition constitutes a dire emergency. The president of the bank that rules the exposition committee's funds must reenter society. Continuing as we have been—segregated from our community and the world that is joining us—is simply not adhering to modern thinking. And Chicago will become a modern city!" He'd pounded his fist on the table. "Do you understand now?"

"I'm sorry, Father. I don't. You will have to teach me," I'd said truthfully.

He'd seemed pleased by my admission. "Of course you couldn't understand. There is so much that needs to be explained to you." He'd leaned forward then and awkwardly patted my hands, which were clenched together in my lap. For far too long his hot, heavy hand rested on mine as his gaze burned into mine. "Thankfully, I am willing to guide you. Not all fathers would be, you know."

"Yes, Father," I'd repeated my rote answer, and tried to still my heart from its frantic beating. "May I pour you more brandy?"

He'd let loose my hands then and nodded. "Yes, indeed. There, you see—you can be guided to learn!"

I'd focused on not spilling the brandy as I poured, but my hands were trembling and the crystal decanter had clanged against his goblet, causing the amber-colored liquor to almost spill. I'd put the bottle down quickly.

"I am sorry, Father. That was awkward of me."

"No matter! You will get more steady with practice." He'd sat back on the velvet divan and sipped his drink, studying me. "I know exactly what you need. I read about it just this morning in the *Tribune*. Seems women's hysteria symptoms are on a rise, and you are obviously suffering from this malady."

Before I could formulate a protest that would not incite him, he'd risen and walked, a little unsteadily, to Mother's small buffet table that sat against the wall and poured from the decanter of red wine that I had, just that morning, watered carefully. He'd brought the crystal wineglass to me and thrust it roughly into my hands, saying, "Drink. The article, written by the acclaimed Doctor Weinstein, stated that one or two glasses per day should be taken as remedy for women's hysteria."

I'd wanted to tell him I was *not* hysterical—that I was lonely and confused and frightened and, yes, angry! Instead I sipped the wine, controlled my expression, and nodded serenely, parroting my "Yes, Father" response.

"You see, that is better. No silly shaking hands for you now!" He'd spoken as if he'd effected a miracle cure.

As I drank the watered wine and watched him chuckle in a self-satisfied manner, I imagined throwing the wine in his pinkish face and bolting from the room, the house, and the life he was trying to thrust me into.

His next words stopped that waking fantasy.

"Two evenings from now, Wednesday night at exactly eight o'clock, will signal the beginning of the reopening of Wheiler House. I have already sent invitations and received assurances all will attend."

My head had felt as if it were going to explode. "Attend? The house reopening?"

"Yes, yes, do try to pay attention, Emily. It won't be a full dinner party, of course. That won't happen until Saturday. On Wednesday we will begin with an intimate group. Just a few close friends—men who also have an interest in the bank, as well as an investment in the World's Columbian Exposition: Burnham, Elcott, Olmsted, Pullman, and Simpton. Five men that I have invited for a light repast. It is an excellent way to move you gently into your new role in society, and, indeed, a very meager party by your mother's standards."

"Two days from *now*? On this Wednesday?" I'd struggled to hold tight to my composure.

"Certainly! We have wasted too much time already by being segregated from the whirlpool of happenings that surround us. The fair opens in two weeks. Wheiler House must be a hub at the center of the wheel that is the new Chicago!"

"But-but I have no idea how to—"

"Oh, it isn't so difficult. And you are a woman, though a young one. Dining and entertaining come naturally to women, and most especially to you."

My face had blazed with heat. "Especially to me?"

"Of course. You are so like your mother."

"What shall I serve? Wear? How shall I—"

"Consult Cook. It isn't as if it's a full dinner party. I already told you that I managed to put that off until Saturday. Three courses should suffice for Wednesday, but be quite certain to have the best of the French cabernet as well as the port brought up from the cellars, and send Carson for more of my cigars. Pullman has an especial fondness for my cigars, though he'd rather smoke mine than buy his own! Ha! A tight millionaire!" He'd drained the last of his brandy and slapped his thighs with his meaty palms. "Oh, and as to what you should wear. You are Lady of Wheiler House and have access to your mother's wardrobe. Make good use of it." He'd lifted his great bulk from the settee and was leaving the room when he'd paused and added, "Wear one of Alice's emerald velvet gowns. It will bring out your eyes."

I wish I could go back to that day and comfort myself by explaining that all that was happening was that the missing pieces of my life were being filled in so that the picture of my future could be complete. I needn't be so frightened and overwhelmed. All would be well—all would be most spectacularly better than well.

But that night I'd had no idea that this small reentry to society would quickly and completely alter my life—I'd only been lost in my fear and loneliness.

Two days passed in a frantic haze for me. Cook and I planned a lobster creamed bisque, a roasted duck breast with asparagus, which was very hard to find this early in the season, and her after-dinner iced vanilla cakes, which Father loved so much.

Mary brought me Mother's collection of emerald velvet gowns. There were more than a dozen of them. She laid them out across my bed like a green waterfall of fabric. I chose the most conservative of them—an evening dress modestly fashioned and unadorned except for pearls sewn into the bodice and the sleeves. Mary clucked her disapproval, muttering that the gold-trimmed gown would make a more dramatic impression. I ignored her and lifted my choice over my head so that she had to assist me into it.

Then the alterations began. I am shorter than Mother, but only slightly, and have a smaller waist. My breasts are larger, though, and when Mary finally helped me lace myself into the gown and I stood before my full-length looking glass, Mary immediately began to cluck and fuss and open seams, trying to contain my flesh.

"All of her dresses will have to be altered, they will," Mary had spoke through a mouthful of pins.

"I don't want to wear Mother's dresses," I'd heard myself saying, which was the truth.

"And why not? They're lovely, and your looks are alike enough to hers that they will be beautiful on you as well. The most of them even more than this one." She'd hesitated, thinking, then while she stared at my bosom and the material stretched tightly there, she added, "Sure and they won't *all* be appropriate as they are made now, but I can find some lace or some silk to add here and there."

As she continued to pin and stitch, my gaze went from the mirror to my own dress that lay in a discarded heap across my bed. It was cream colored and lacey and covered with blushing pink rosebuds, and it was as different from Mother's fine velvet gowns as was Mary's brown linen uniform dress from Lady Astor's day dresses.

Yes, of course I'd known then, as now, that I should have been delighted by the vast addition to my wardrobe. Mother had been one of the finest dressed women in Chicago. But when my gaze made its way back to the mirror, the girl swathed in her mother's gown who looked out at me felt like a stranger, and me—Emily—had seemed to be utterly lost somewhere in her unfamiliar reflection.

When I wasn't talking with Cook or standing for alterations or trying to remember the endless details of entertaining that Mother had mastered with what had seemed like no effort at all, I wandered silently through our huge mansion, trying to avoid Father and speaking to no one. Odd how I'd not thought of our home as huge until after Mother was no longer filling it. But with her gone it had become an enormous cage, filled with all of the beautiful things one woman had collected, including her only living child.

Living child? Before that Wednesday evening, I had started to believe that I had quit living and I was only existing as a shell, waiting for my body to catch me up and realize that I was already dead.

Miraculously it was then that Arthur Simpton brought me back to life!

This evening, Wednesday, the nineteenth of April, Father sent a glass of wine up to my dressing room as Mary readied me for my first social event as Lady of Wheiler House. I knew the wine was strong, unwatered from the special bottles Father had ordered up from the wine cellar. I'd sipped it while Mary combed and pinned my thick auburn hair into place.

"'Tis a considerate man, he is, your father," Mary had chattered. "It warms my heart, it does, how much care and attention he's been showin' ye."

I hadn't said anything. What could I have said? I could easily look through her eyes at me, and at Father. Of course he appeared careful and considerate of me to the outside world—they had never seen his burning look or felt the unbearable heat of his hand!

When my coiffure was done Mary had stepped away. I'd stood

from the chair at my vanity and walked to my full-length looking glass. I'll never forget that first sight of myself as a woman fully grown. My cheeks had been flushed from the wine, which came easily to me as my skin is so fair—as fair as Mother's had been. The dress fit me as if it had always been mine. It was the exact color of our eyes.

I stared and thought hopelessly, *I am my mother,* at the same instant Mary whispered, "You are so like her, 'tis like seein' a ghost," and crossed herself.

There was a knock on my dressing room door and Carson's voice announced, "Miss Wheiler, your father sends word that the gentlemen have begun to arrive."

"Yes. All right. I'll come down in a moment." I hadn't moved, though. I don't believe I could have made my body move had Mary not gently squeezed my hand and said, "There now, I was silly to speak so. 'Tis not your mother's ghost you are. Not at all. 'Tis a lovely lass who does credit to her memory. I'll light a candle for ye tonight and pray her spirit watches over ye and gives you strength." Then she'd opened the door for me, and I'd had no choice but to leave the room, and my childhood, behind.

It was a long way from my third-floor bedchamber and private parlor that had begun as a spacious nursery for children that never came, but it seemed it took only an instant for me to reach the last landing—the one that opened to the first-floor foyer below. I'd paused there. The deep male voices that lifted to me sounded odd and out of place in a home that had been so silent for so many months.

"Ah, there you are, Emily." Father had closed the few steps between us, joining me on the landing. Formally, he bowed and then, as I'd seen him do for Mother countless times, held out his arm for me to take it. I automatically rested my hand on his arm and moved down the remainder of the staircase beside him. I could feel his eyes on me. "You are a picture, my dear. A picture." I'd looked up at him then, surprised to hear the familiar compliment he'd paid Mother so many times.

I hated the way he was looking at me. Even after the joy the rest of the evening brought me, that hatred is still fresh in my mind. He studied me ravenously. It was as if I were one of the rare cuts of lamb on which he habitually gorged himself.

I still wonder if any of the waiting men that evening noticed Father's terrible gaze, and my stomach roils with sickness at the thought of it.

His gaze left me and he beamed effusively at the small gathering of men below us. "You see, Simpton. Nothing to worry about at all. Emily is right as rain—right as rain."

I'd looked down, expecting to see a graying man with rheumy eyes, a thick walrus mustache, and a barrel chest, but my eyes met the clear, blue gaze of a dashingly handsome young man who was smiling good-naturedly at me.

"Arthur!" His name had escaped before I could control my words.

His brilliant blue eyes had crinkled at the corners with his smile, but before he could respond, Father cut in gruffly. "Emily, there will be no overfamiliarity tonight, especially when Simpton here is standing in for his father."

I felt my face flame with heat.

"Mr. Wheiler, I'm sure it was surprise that caused your daughter to speak so familiarly. I am, alas, not the man my father is," he'd joked, puffing up his cheeks and swelling his chest as to mimic his father's girth. "Or at least not yet!"

A man I easily recognized as Mr. Pullman slapped Arthur on the back and laughed heartily. "Your father does have a love of good food. Can't say I'm not guilty of the same." He patted his own impressive belly.

Carson chose then to step from an arched doorway and call, "Dinner is served, Miss Wheiler."

It had taken me several moments to realize that Carson was actually speaking to me. I swallowed past the dryness in my throat and said, "Gentlemen, if you will follow me to the dining room we would be honored by your company for tonight's modest repast." Father had nodded his approval to me and we'd begun walking toward the formal dining room when I couldn't stop myself from peeking back over my shoulder for another glimpse of Arthur Simpton.

And I stumbled into Mr. Pullman's impressive girth.

"Alice, do watch where you are walking!" Father had snapped.

When he spoke I had been readying an apology for Mr. Pullman, so I saw the older man's face as he registered the fact that my father had just called me by my dead mother's name. His concern was palpable. "Oh, Barrett, think nothing of it! Your lovely and talented *daughter* may stumble into me at will." The dear man put his hand on Father's shoulder, gently guiding him ahead of me, all the while engaging him in conversation and moving him forward into the dining room so that I could pause and have a moment to collect myself. "Now, let us discuss an idea I have for adding electric lighting to Central Station. I believe the night traffic that will be generated by the Columbian Exposition justifies the expense, which we can more than make up for in the additional train tickets sold. You know I hold controlling shares in the station. I would be willing to . . ."

Pullman's voice trailed away as he and Father strode into the dining room. I'd stood there, frozen as stone, the words *Alice, do watch where you are walking!* playing round and round in my mind.

"May I escort you to dinner, Miss Wheiler?"

I looked up into Arthur Simpton's kind blue eyes. "Y-yes, please, sir," I'd managed.

He'd offered his arm, and I placed my hand on it. Unlike my

father's, Arthur's forearm was trim, and there was no dark mat of hair tufting out from under his cuffed dress shirt. And he was so delightfully tall!

"Don't worry," he'd whispered as we led the rest of the small group into the dining room. "No one except Pullman and I heard him call you Alice."

My gaze had darted up to his.

"It was an understandable mistake," he continued, speaking quickly and quietly for my ears only. "But I know it must have been painful for you."

It was difficult for me to speak, so I only nodded.

"Then I will attempt to distract you from your pain."

And a wondrous thing happened—Arthur positioned himself beside me at dinner! I was, of course, sitting to Father's right, but his attention—for once—was utterly distracted from me by Mr. Pullman on his left and Mr. Burnham, who was sitting beside Mr. Pullman. When their discussion turned from the electricity at Central Station to the lighting of the Midway of the exposition, the architect, Mr. Frederick Law Olmsted, joined the conversation, adding even more passion to the argument. Arthur stayed out of much of the conversation. At first the other men joked that he was a poor stand-in for his gout-ridden father, but he laughed and agreed; then when they returned to their battle of words, Arthur returned his attention to me.

No one seemed to notice, not even Father, at least not after I called for the fifth bottle of our good cabernet to be opened and liberally poured—though he did send me a sharp look if I laughed at one of Arthur's witticisms. I learned quickly to stifle my laughter and instead smile shyly at my plate.

I did look up, though, as often as I dared. I wanted to look into Arthur's beautiful blue eyes and see the sparkle and the kindness with which they watched me.

But I did not want Father to see, nor did I want Mr. Elcott to see.

Mr. Elcott's gaze did not have my father's intensity, but I did find it on me often that night. It reminded me that Mrs. Elcott, as well as Camille, expected that Arthur Simpton was close to declaring his serious affections for their daughter, though in complete honesty I will admit that I did not need a reminder.

As I write this I do feel a measure of sadness, or perhaps pity is the more sincere emotion, for poor Camille. But she should not have deluded herself. The truth is the truth. That night I took nothing from her that she hadn't attempted to first take from me.

I also took nothing that was not freely, joyfully, given.

The dinner that I had dreaded seemed to last but a fleeting moment. Too soon, Father, his face flushed and his words slurred, pushed back from the table, stood, and announced, "Let us retire to my library for brandy and cigars."

I'd stood when Father did, and the other five men got instantly to their feet.

"Let us first have a toast," Mr. Pullman had said. He'd lifted his mostly empty wineglass, and the rest of the men had followed suit. "To Miss Emily Wheiler for a delightful dinner. You are a credit to your mother."

"To Miss Wheiler!" the men said, raising their glasses to me.

I am not ashamed to admit that I'd felt a rush of pride and of happiness. "Thank you, gentlemen. You are all most kind." As they all bowed to me I managed to sneak a look at Arthur, who winked quickly and flashed a handsome, white-toothed smile at me.

"My dear, you were a picture tonight—a picture," Father slurred. "Have brandy and cigars sent to my library."

"Thank you, Father," I'd said softly. "And I already arranged for George to be waiting in your library with both brandy and cigars."

He'd taken my hand in his. His was large and moist, as it always was, and he lifted mine to his lips. "You have done well tonight. I bid you a good night, my dear."

The other men had echoed his good-night wishes, as I hurried from the room, wiping the back of my hand on my voluminous velvet skirts. I'd felt my father's gaze burning me the whole way and I did not dare look back, even for one last glimpse of Arthur Simpton.

I'd started toward the stairs, meaning to secret myself in my bedchamber so that I would be well out of sight when Father, thoroughly drunk, stumbled to his bed. I'd even told Mary, who was chattering nonstop about what a success I'd been, to give me just a few moments to myself, but then I'd be ready for her to come to my room and help me out of the intricacies of Mother's gown so that I may change into my nightgown for bed.

As I consider back on it, tonight it seemed as if my body was completely in control of my actions, and my mind could do nothing except to follow its lead.

My feet had detoured around the wide staircase and I'd slipped quietly down the servants' hall and out the rear door where my hands had lifted my mother's skirts and I'd almost flown to the quiet bench under the willow tree that I had made my own.

Once I reached the dark security of my special place, my mind had begun to reason once again. Yes, Father should be smoking and drinking with the other men for hours, so it was logical that I could hide safely away there for most of the night. But I'd understood it would be too dangerous to stay but a few moments. What if the moment I chose to slip upstairs was the same moment Father stumbled from his library to relieve himself or to bellow for the cook to bring him something to satisfy his insatiable appetite? No. No. I would not chance that. And, of course, there was Mary. She would look for me if she didn't find me in my bedchamber, and I did not want even Mary to discover my sanctuary.

Still, I'd breathed a deep, satisfied breath, taking in the cool night air and feeling the comfort lent to me by the concealing shadows. I'd wanted to steal just a few moments for myself—a few moments here, in my special place, to think about Arthur Simpton.

He'd shown me such special kindness! It had been so long since I'd laughed, and even though I'd had to stifle my giggles, I had still felt them! Arthur Simpton had transformed the evening I had so dreaded from a strange and frightening event to the most magical dinner I had ever experienced.

I hadn't wanted it to end. I still do not want it to end.

I remember that I could not contain myself for another moment. I stood, and holding wide my arms I twirled around in the darkness within the curtain of willow boughs and laughed joyously until, exhausted by the unaccustomed rush of emotion, I sank to the young grass, breathing hard and brushing from my face the thick fall of hair that had escaped my chignon.

"You should never stop laughing. When you do, your beauty changes from extraordinary to divine and you look like a goddess come to earth to tempt us with your untouchable loveliness."

I'd scrambled to my feet, more thrilled than shocked as Arthur Simpton parted the willow boughs and stepped within.

"Mr. Simpton! I-I did not realize anyone was—"

"Mr. Simpton?" He'd cut me off with a warm, contagious smile. "Surely even your father would agree we need not be so formal here."

My heart had been pounding so loudly that I believe it drowned out the sound of my good sense that was shouting at me to hold my words, smile, and return quickly inside, because instead of doing any of those three reasonable things, I'd blurted, "My father would not agree to us being alone in the garden together, no matter what I call you."

Arthur's smile had instantly dimmed. "Does your father disapprove of me?"

I shook my head. "No, no, it is nothing like that—or at least I don't believe so. It is just that since Mother's death, Father seems to disapprove of everything."

"I am sure that is because he has so recently lost his wife."

"As I have so recently lost my mother!" I'd had enough sense remaining to me to press my lips together in a tight line and stop my outburst. Beginning to feel nervous, and incredibly clumsy, I'd walked to the marble bench and sat, trying to tidy my escaping hair, as I'd continued, "Forgive me, Mr. Simpton. I shouldn't have spoken to you like that."

"Why ever not! Can we not be friends, Emily?" He'd followed me to the bench, but did not sit beside me.

"Yes," I'd said softly, glad my errant hair hid my face. "I would like us to be friends."

"Then you must call me Arthur and feel free to speak to me as you would a friend, and I will have to be certain your father finds nothing at all to disapprove of about me. I won't even mention to him that I discovered you in the garden."

My hands had instantly stilled and dropped from my hair. "Please, Arthur. If you are my friend, promise me you will not mention that you saw me after I left the dining room."

I thought I saw what might have been surprise in his deep blue eyes, but it was replaced too soon by a kind, reassuring smile for me to have been sure. "Emily, I will say nothing of tonight to your father except to repeat what a lovely hostess his daughter was."

"Thank you, Arthur."

He did sit beside me then. Not close, but his scent came to me—cigars and something that was almost sweet. Thinking back I realize that was foolish. How could a man smell of sweetness? But I didn't know him well enough yet to understand that the absence of strong spirits and cigars on his breath seemed sweet after Father's foul odor.

"Do you come here often?" His question had seemed such an easy one to answer.

"Yes, I do."

"And your father doesn't know you do?"

I'd hesitated only a moment. His eyes were so kind—his gaze so honest—and he said he'd wanted to be my friend. Surely I could confide in him, but perhaps I should do so carefully. I'd shrugged nonchalantly and found an answer that was as truthful as it was vague. "Oh, Father is so busy with business that he rarely even notices the gardens."

"But you like them?"

I'd nodded. "I do. They're beautiful."

"At night? But it's so dark and you are so very alone."

"Well, as you are my friend now I feel I can tell you a secret, even though it may not be very ladylike." I'd smiled shyly up at him.

Arthur grinned mischievously. "Is it your secret that isn't ladylike, or the telling of it to me?"

"I am afraid perhaps it is both." My shyness had begun to evaporate, and I'd even dared to lower my lashes coquettishly.

"Now I am intrigued. As your friend, I insist you tell me." He'd leaned a little toward me.

I'd met his eyes and trusted him with the truth. "I like the darkness. It's friendly and comforting."

His smile had dimmed, and I'd worried that I truly had let my words reveal too much. But when he spoke his voice had lost none of his kindness. "Poor Emily, I can imagine you've needed to be comforted these past months, and if this garden comforts you, day or night, then I say it is a wondrous place indeed!"

I'd felt a rush of relief, and of joy at his empathy. "Yes, you see, it is my escape and my oasis. Close your eyes and breathe deeply. You'll forget that it's night."

"Well, all right. I will." He'd closed his eyes and drew a deep breath. "What is that lovely scent? I didn't notice it until now."

"It's the stargazer lilies. They've just begun to bloom," I'd explained happily. "No, keep your eyes closed. Now, listen. Tell me what you hear."

"Your voice, which sounds to me as sweet as the lilies smell."

His compliment made my head light, but I'd scolded him with mock seriousness. "Not me, Arthur. Listen to the silence and tell me what you hear within it."

He'd kept his eyes closed, tilted his head, and said, "Water. I hear the fountain."

"Exactly! I especially like sitting here, hidden under this willow. It is as if I have found my own world where I can hear the sound of the water rushing from the fountain and imagine that I'm riding my bicycle again beside the lake with the wind in my hair and no one and nothing catching me."

Arthur opened his eyes and met my gaze. "No one? No one at all? Not even a special friend?"

My whole body had felt flushed and I'd said, "Perhaps now I could imagine a friend joining me, and I do remember how you love to bicycle."

He'd surprised me then by slapping his forehead. "Bicycle! That reminds me of how I found you here in the garden. I excused myself early so that I might return home to speak to Father before he goes to bed. I'd bicycled here, and was alone, mounting my bicycle to return home when I heard laughter." He'd paused, and his voice had deepened. "It was the most beautiful laughter I had ever in my life heard. It seemed to be coming from the grounds behind the house. I saw the garden gate, opened it, and followed the sound to you."

"Oh." I'd breathed the word on a happy sigh, my face feeling even warmer. I'd said, "I am glad my laughter brought you to me."

"Emily, your laughter didn't simply bring me to you—it drew me to you."

"I have another secret I could tell you," I'd heard myself saying.

"Then that is another secret I will keep and treasure as my own," he'd said.

"When I was laughing, I was thinking about how happy I was that you had been at dinner. I had been so terribly nervous before you sat beside me." I'd held my breath, hoping I had not been what Mother would have called too forward with him.

"Well, then, I am very, very pleased to announce that I will be returning to your home for your dinner party Saturday, and that I will be escorting a lovely woman with whom I hope you will also become fast friends."

My heart, already so battered and bruised, ached at his words. But I was learning the lesson of hiding my feelings well, so I put on the same interested expression and soft voice I used with Father and said, "Oh, how nice. It will be good to see Camille again. You should know she and I are already friends."

"Camille?" He'd looked utterly baffled. And then I could see his expression shift to understanding. "Oh, you mean Samuel Elcott's daughter, Camille."

"Well, yes, of course," I'd said, but already my bruised heart was beating more easily.

"Of course? Why do you say 'of course'?"

"I thought it was understood that you were interested in courting Camille," I'd said, and then felt my heart become lighter and lighter as he shook his head and replied with an empathic, "I don't know how something I have no knowledge of could be *understood*."

I'd felt as if I should say something in defense of what I knew would be poor Camille's great embarrassment had she heard

Arthur's words. "I believe the *understanding* was something Mrs. Elcott was hoping for."

Arthur's dark brows lifted, along with the corners of his lips. "Well, then let me make *your* understanding clear. I will be escorting my mother to your dinner party on Saturday. My father's gout is plaguing him, but Mother wishes to attend your first true social event in support of you. She is the friend I was hoping you would make."

"So, you will not be courting Camille?" I'd asked boldly, though breathlessly.

Arthur stood then and, smiling, bowed formally to me. In a voice filled with warmth and kindness, he'd announced, "Miss Emily Wheiler, I can assure you it is not Camille Elcott I will be courting. And now I must, reluctantly, bid you a good night until Saturday."

He'd turned and left me breathless with happiness and expectation, and it had seemed to me that even the shadows around me reflected my joy with their beautiful, concealing mantle of darkness.

But I hadn't spent many more moments reveling in the magical events of the night. Though my heart was filled by Arthur Simpton and I wanted to think of nothing but our wondrous conversation and that he had practically left me with a promise that it would be me he would be courting in the future, my mind was cataloging the other, less romantic information Arthur had just provided me. Though my hands shake with joy as, safely in my room, I relive through this journal my meeting with Arthur, and begin to imagine what a future with him could bring, I must remember to be very quiet when I come to my garden spot.

I must not ever draw *anyone else there.*

April 27th, 1893
Emily Wheiler's Journal

I begin this journal entry with trepidation. I can feel myself changing. I hope the change is for the better, but I confess that I am not certain it is. Actually, if I am to write with complete honesty, I must admit that even hope has changed its meaning for me.

I am so confused! And so very, very afraid.

Of only one thing am I sure, and that is that I must escape Wheiler House by any means possible. Arthur Simpton has provided me a logical and safe escape, and I have accepted him.

I am not the giddy child I was eight days ago, after that first night Arthur and I spoke. I still find him kind and charming and, of course, handsome. I believe I could love him. A beautiful future is within my grasp, so why is it that I feel a growing coldness within me? Has the fear and loathing I have for Father begun to taint me?

I shudder at the thought.

Perhaps as I review the events of the past days, I will find the answers to my questions.

Arthur's garden visit had, indeed, changed my world. Suddenly, the Saturday dinner party was no longer something I dreaded—it was something I counted down the hours to. I threw myself into the menu, the decorations, and every tiny detail of my gown.

What was going to be a five-course dinner that I'd uncaringly told Cook to resurrect from one of Mother's old party books utterly changed. Instead, I raked through my memories, wishing I had paid better attention—*any* attention really—when Mother and Father had discussed the especially sumptuous social dinners they'd attended in the year before she had had to withdraw from society because of her pregnancy. Finally, I recalled how even Father had praised a particular dinner at the University Club that had been sponsored by his bank and held in honor of the exposition architects. I sent Mary, whose sister was one of the University Club's legion of cooks, to get a copy of the menu—and then I was pleasantly surprised when she actually did return with a list of not simply the courses, but the wines that should accompany them. Cook, who I believe until then had mostly pitied and humored my attempts at menu making, began to look at me with respect.

Next, I changed the table settings and decorations. I wanted to bring the garden inside, to remind Arthur of our time together, so I supervised the gardeners in cutting bushels of fragrant stargazer lilies from our gardens—though not from around the fountain. I also ordered them to gather cattails from the marshy area around the lakeshore, as well as curtains of ivy. Then I set about filling vases and vases with lilies, cattails, and trailing ivy, hoping all the while that Arthur would notice.

And while I was in the center of a whirlwind of activity of my own creation, I realized something incredibly interesting—the more demanding I became, the more the people about me complied. Where once I had tiptoed around Wheiler House, the timid ghost of the girl I used to be, now I strode purposefully, calling out commands with confidence.

I continue to learn. This lesson is one I'm finding most important. There may be a better way of ordering the world around me than my mother's way. She used her beauty and her soft, pleasing voice to coax, cajole, and get her way. I am discovering that I prefer a stronger approach.

Is that wrong of me? Is that part of the coldness I feel spreading within me? How can gaining confidence and control be wrong?

Whether right or wrong, I used my newly discovered knowledge when I chose my gown. Father had, of course, commanded me to wear one of Mother's green velvet gowns again.

I refused.

Oh, I was not foolish enough to refuse him outright. I simply rejected every one of my mother's green velvet dresses Mary offered me. Where before she would have insisted until I capitulated, my new attitude and bearing had her befuddled.

"But, lass, you must wear one of your mother's gowns. Your father has been quite firm about it," she'd protested one last time.

"I will follow Father's request, but it will be on my own terms. I am the Lady of Wheiler House and not a child's doll to be dressed up." I'd gone to my armoire and pulled from the recesses of it the gown I had planned on wearing for my Presentation Ball. It was cream silk with cascades of embroidered green ivy decorating the skirt. The bodice, though modest, was full, as was the skirt, but the waist was synched tiny, so that my figure became a perfect hourglass. And my arms were left alluringly, though appropriately, bare. I handed the gown to Mary. "Take a green velvet sash and bow from one of Mother's dresses. I'll wrap the sash around my waist, and stitch the bow to the side of the bodice. And bring me one of her green velvet hair ribbons. I'll wear it tied around my neck. If Father objects, I can truthfully tell him that I am, as he asked, wearing Mother's green velvet."

Mary frowned and muttered to herself, but she did as I told her to do. Everyone did as I told them to do. Even Father was subdued when I refused to go to the GFWC on Friday, saying that I was simply too busy.

"Well, Emily, tomorrow everything must be just so—just so. Skipping this week's volunteer duties is certainly understandable. It is commendable to see you fulfilling your responsibilities as Lady of Wheiler House."

"Thank you, Father." I'd answered him with the same words I used countless times before, but hadn't softened my tone and dropped my head. Instead, I looked him directly in the eye, and added, "And I won't be able to dine with you this evening. There is just too much for me to do and time is too short."

"Indeed, well, indeed. Be quite certain you make good use of your time, Emily."

"Oh, do not worry, Father. I will."

Nodding to himself, Father hadn't seemed to notice that I'd left the room before he'd dismissed me.

It had been a delicious luxury to command George to bring a tray up to my sitting room Friday evening. I ate in perfect peace, sipped a small glass of wine, and recounted the gold-foiled RSVPs— all twenty invitations had, indeed, been accepted.

I had placed the Simptons' reply card on the top of the pile.

Then I lounged on my daybed that sat before my small, third-floor balcony, and burned six pillared candlesticks while I leafed through the latest Montgomery Ward catalog. For the first time I began to believe I might enjoy being Lady of Wheiler House.

Excitement didn't keep me from feeling a dizzying rush of nerves when Carson made his announcement Saturday evening that the guests were beginning to arrive. I'd taken one final look in the mirror while Mary tied the thin velvet ribbon around my neck.

"You are a great beauty, lass," Mary had told me. "You will be a success tonight."

I'd lifted my chin and spoke to my reflection, banishing the ghost of my mother. "Yes, I will."

When I'd reached the landing, Father's back was to me. He was already engaged in an animated conversation with Mr. Pullman and Mr. Ryerson. Carson was opening the front door for several couples. Two women—one I recognized as the rather plump Mrs. Pullman, and the other, a taller, more handsome woman—were admiring the large central arrangement of lilies, cattails, and draping ivy I'd spent so many hours on. Raised in pleasure, their voices had carried easily to me.

"Well, this is quite lovely and unusual," Mrs. Pullman said.

The taller woman had nodded appreciatively. "What an excellent choice to use these lilies. They have filled the foyer with an exquisite scent. It is as if we entered a fragrant indoor garden."

I hadn't moved. I'd wanted to take a private moment of pleasure, so I'd imagined, just for an instant, that I was back on my bench in the garden, curtained by willows, cloaked by darkness, and sitting beside Arthur Simpton. I'd closed my eyes, drawn a deep breath, inhaling calm, and as I released it his voice had lifted to me, as if carried on the power of my imaginings.

"There is Miss Wheiler herself. Mother, I do believe the arrangement you have been admiring shows evidence of her hand."

I'd opened my eyes to gaze down at Arthur, standing beside the handsome women I hadn't recognized. I'd smiled, said, "Good evening Mr. Simpton," and had begun descending the last flight of stairs. Father had brushed past them and hurried to meet me, moving so quickly that he was puffing with effort when he offered me his arm.

"Emily, I do not believe you have met Arthur's mother, Mrs. Simpton," Father said, presenting me to her.

"Miss Wheiler, you are even more lovely than my son described," Mrs. Simpton had said. "And this centerpiece arrangement of yours is spectacular. Did you, as my son surmised, create it yourself?"

"Yes, Mrs. Simpton, I did. And I am flattered that you admire it." I hadn't been able to stop myself from smiling up at Arthur as I spoke. His kind blue eyes were alight with his own smile—one I was already finding familiar and increasingly dear.

"And how would you know Emily created the arrangement?" I'd been stunned by the gruff tone of Father's voice, sure that everyone around us could hear the possessiveness in it.

Nonplused, Arthur laughed good-naturedly. "Well, I recognize the stargazer lilies from—" Partway through his explanation, he must have seen the horror in my eyes because he broke off his words with an exaggerated cough.

"Son, are you well?" His mother had touched his arm in concern.

Arthur had cleared his throat and regained his smile. "Oh, quite well, Mother. Just a tickle in my throat."

"What is it you were saying about Emily's flowers?" Father had been like a bloated old dog with a bone.

Arthur hadn't missed a beat, but had continued smoothly, "Are they Emily's flowers? Then I have made an excellent guess because they instantly reminded me of her. They, too, are exceptionally beautiful as well as sweet."

"Oh, Arthur, you do sound more and more like your father every day." Arthur's mother had squeezed his arm with obvious affection.

"Arthur! Oh, my. I had hoped you would be here." Camille had rushed up to us, ahead of her mother, though Mrs. Elcott followed so closely on her daughter's heels that it appeared as if she pushed her along.

"Miss Elcott." Arthur had bowed stiffly, formally. "Mrs. Elcott, good evening. I am escorting my mother as my father is still unwell."

"What a coincidence! My Camille joins me this evening because Mr. Elcott believes he may be coming down with an ague. And, of course, I so wanted to be sure I was here to support Emily at her first formal dinner as Lady of Wheiler House that I couldn't bear to cancel." Mrs. Elcott had explained with a honeyed tone, but her pinched expression as she cast her gaze from Arthur to me belied her words. "Though, sadly, I have only daughters and no devoted son. You are a fortunate mother, Mrs. Simpton."

"Oh, I readily agree with you, Mrs. Elcott," Arthur's mother had said with a fond smile. "He is a devoted and an observant son. We were just discussing that it was he who guessed that these lovely decorations were created by Miss Wheiler herself."

"Emily? You did that?"

Camille had sounded so shocked that I'd had a sudden urge to slap her. Instead I lifted my chin and did not soften my voice and make little of my accomplishments, as Mother would have.

"Hello, Camille, what a surprise it is to see you. And, yes, I did make this arrangement. I also created all of the arrangements on the dining table, as well as those in Father's library."

"You are a credit to me, my dear," Father had said.

I'd ignored him and kept my focus on Camille, and very precisely said, "As you and your mother observed during your last visit, I am learning early what it is to be the Lady of a great house." I had not added the rest of what Mrs. Elcott had said, *which is something my future husband will be glad of*. I hadn't needed to. I'd simply needed to turn my gaze from Camille to Arthur, and then return the warm smile he'd been beaming at me.

"Yes, well, as I said. You are a credit to me." Father offered his arm to me again. I'd had to take it. He nodded to the Simptons and El-cotts, saying, "And now we must greet the rest of our guests. Emily, I do not see the champagne being served."

"That is because I chose to follow the University Club's lead with the menu tonight. George will be serving amontillado before the first course instead of champagne. It will pair much better with the fresh oysters."

"Very good, very good. Let us find some of that amontillado, my dear. Ah, I see the Ayers have arrived. There is talk of a permanent art collection for his Indian relics, which the bank will be very inter-ested in . . ."

I'd stopped listening, though I allowed Father to lead me away with him. That entire night, as I played the part of hostess and Lady of Wheiler House, I kept always in my mind the hope that Arthur Simpton was noticing, and each time I managed to steal a look at him our eyes met because *he had been watching me*. His smile had seemed to say he had also been appreciating me.

As the evening progressed, I'd understood that, as always, after dinner the men would leave us and retire to Father's library for brandy and cigars. The women would go to Mother's formal parlor, sip iced wine, nibble on tea cakes and, of course, gossip. I'd dreaded that separation, and not simply because Arthur would not be there, but because I had no experience conversing with ladies of my mother's age. Camille was the only one of them within a decade of my age. I'd realized I had a choice to make. I could sit beside Camille and chatter like I was nothing more than any other young girl, or I could truly attempt to be Lady of Wheiler House. I knew I might be treated with condescension. There were, after all, great ladies such as Mrs. Ryerson, Mrs. Pullman, and Mrs. Ayer present, and I was but a sixteen-year-old girl. But as I led the ladies into Mother's parlor, and was met with the familiar and soothing scent of the stargazers I had so meticulously arranged, I made my choice. I did not withdraw to the window seat with Camille and cling to my childhood. Instead, I took Mother's position in the center of the room on the divan, supervised Mary's refreshing of the ladies' wine, and tried to hold my chin up and think of something—anything intelligent—to say into the building silence.

Arthur's mother was my salvation.

"Miss Wheiler, I am interested in these unusual bouquet creations you have beautifully displayed in each of the rooms. Would you share with me your inspiration?" she'd asked with a warm smile that had reminded me so much of her son's.

"Yes, dear," I'd been amazed to hear Mrs. Ayer say. "The decorations are quite cunning. You must share your secret with us."

"I was inspired by our gardens and by the fountain at its heart. I wanted to bring the lily scent and the water imagery, and my favorite tree, the willow, inside tonight."

"Oh, I see! The cattails evoke the presence of water," Mrs. Simpton had said.

"And the trailing ivy is arranged much like the fronds of a willow," Mrs. Ayer had said, nodding in obvious appreciation. "That was an excellent idea."

"Emily, I haven't known you to be particularly fond of the garden. I thought you and Camille were much more concerned with bicycling and the latest Gibson Girl styles than gardening." Mrs. Elcott had spoken with the exact tone of condescension I had been dreading.

For a moment I said nothing. There had seemed to be a breathless silence in the room, as if the house itself awaited my response. Would I be a girl or a lady?

I straightened my back, lifted my chin, and met Mrs. Elcott's patronizing gaze. "Indeed, Mrs. Elcott, I have enjoyed bicycling and Gibson Girl styles, but that was when my mother, your particular friend, was Lady of Wheiler House. She is dead. I have had to step into her role, and I find that I must be concerned with things that are not so girlish." I'd heard clucks of concern and several of the women whispered *the poor thing*. That further emboldened me, and I'd realized how I could use Mrs. Elcott's condescension to my favor. I'd continued, "I know I cannot hope to be as great a lady as Mother was, but I have resolved to do my best. I can only hope that Mother is looking down on me with pride." I'd sniffed delicately and used my lace napkin to dab the corners of my eyes.

"Oh, you sweet girl." Mrs. Simpton had patted my shoulder. "As your father said earlier, you are a credit to your family. Your mother and I were not well acquainted, but I am a mother with daughters of my own, so I feel confident when I say that she would be very proud of you, very proud indeed!"

Then each of the ladies, in turn, consoled me and assured me of their admiration. Each of the ladies except Mrs. and Miss Elcott. Camille and her mother said little for the rest of the evening, and were the first of my guests to leave.

An hour or so later, when the men came to collect their women, conversation flowed in my parlor as freely as brandy had obviously flowed in Father's library. Our guests bade us effusive good nights, praising everything about the evening.

Arthur and his mother were the last to depart.

"Mr. Wheiler, it has been quite some time since I have had such an agreeable evening," Mrs. Simpton told Father, as he bowed to her. "And I do so appreciate it, as I have been uncommonly worried about my good husband's health. But your daughter was such an attentive hostess that I feel my spirits have been lifted."

"Pleasantly said, pleasantly said," Father had slurred, weaving a little as he stood beside me just within the foyer.

"Please, Madam, send Mr. Simpton my best wishes for a swift recovery," I'd said, holding my breath in hopeful anticipation of her next words.

"Well, you must call on Mr. Simpton yourself!" Arthur's mother had exclaimed, just as I'd wished her to. "You would be such a lovely diversion for him, especially as he desperately misses our two daughters. They are both married and remained in New York with their husbands' families."

"I would enjoy calling on you very much," I'd said, touching Father's arm and adding, "Father, do you not think it would be a kindness to visit Mr. and Mrs. Simpton, as he has been so unwell?"

"Yes, yes, of course," Father had said, nodding dismissively.

"Excellent. Then I shall send Arthur around with our carriage on Monday afternoon."

"Arthur? The carriage? I do not—" Father had begun but Mrs. Simpton had interrupted, nodding her head as if she agreed with whatever edict he was getting ready to speak. "I do not like the current craze of young people bicycling everywhere, either. And those bloomers girls are wearing—atrocious!" Mrs. Simpton had leveled her gaze on her son. "Arthur, I know that you are fond of your bicycle, but Mr. Wheiler and I insist his daughter travels in a more civilized manner. Do we not, Mr. Wheiler?"

"Indeed," Father had agreed. "Bicycles are not appropriate for ladies."

"Precisely! So my son will take the carriage for Miss Wheiler on Monday afternoon. It is well decided. Good night!" Mrs. Simpton had taken her son's arm. Arthur bowed formally to Father, bidding him good night. When he turned to me his bow was just as formal, but his gaze met mine and his quick wink was for me alone.

As soon as the door closed I went into action. I'd recognized Father's weaving and slurring. My heart was too filled with the success of the evening and the obvious attentions being paid me by Arthur and his mother. I'd not wanted to take any chance that Father would ruin my happiness with his alcohol breath, his hot, heavy hands, and his burning gaze.

"I'll wish you a good night now, Father," I'd said with a quick curtsey. "I must see that everything is back in its proper place tonight, and it is already so late. Carson!" I'd called and then had breathed a great sigh of relief when Father's valet hurried into the foyer. "Please help Father to his bedchamber."

Then I'd turned and, with purposeful, confident strides, retreated from the room.

And Father hadn't called me back!

I'd been so giddy with victory that I practically danced into the dining room where, just as I'd already directed, George was putting everything back to order.

"Leave the flower arrangements, George," I'd directed him. "The scent really is spectacular."

"Yes, Miss."

Mary was tidying the parlor. "You can leave that for now. I'd rather have you help me out of this gown. I am exhausted."

"Yes, Miss," had been her response, as well.

Had I actually ended the night after Mary had helped me into my sleep chemise, I would be recording that as the most perfect evening of my life. Sadly, I was too restless for sleep—too restless to even write of the evening's events in my journal. I'd craved the comfort of my sweet, familiar garden, and the soothing touch of the darkness that brought me a special sense of calm.

I'd wrapped my night robe around me and, on slippered feet I'd padded silently, swiftly, down the wide stairway. I heard the servants distantly in the kitchen, but no one saw me as I slipped from the house and into my gardens.

It had been late—much later than I usually ventured outside, but the moon was more than half full, and my feet knew their way. My willow awaited me. Under its curtained darkness I curled up on the marble bench, gazed at the fountain, and then, like each memory was a jewel, I sifted through the events of the evening.

Arthur Simpton's mother had made it clear that she prefers me! It had even seemed that she and her son were in cahoots, and that they worked together to slip around Father's possessive disapproval.

I'd wanted to stand and dance and laugh with joy, but Arthur had taught me a valuable lesson. I had no intention of anyone, not even one of the servants, discovering my special place, so I remained quietly on the bench and imagined myself dancing and laughing in joy under my willow tree, and I promised myself then that someday I would be Lady of my own great house, and my Lord and husband would have kind blue eyes and a warm smile.

As I write this, remembering the evening, I do not believe my manipulations malicious. Arthur and his mother had paid me special attention. Was it wrong that I wanted to use their affections to escape a situation I was finding more and more difficult to bear?

The answer I find is no. I would be good to Arthur. I would be close to his mother. I was not doing an evil act by encouraging the Simptons.

But I digress. I must continue to report the horrific events that followed.

That night, the comfortable shadows beneath my willow tree had worked their usual magic. My mind had ceased its whirring and I'd felt a lovely sleepiness come over me. Almost as if I was in a waking dream, I'd slowly, languidly, left the gardens and made my way back through the dark, silent house. I was yawning widely when I reached the second-floor landing. I'd covered my mouth to stifle the sound when Father stepped from the unlit hallway.

"What are you doing?" His words were rough, and came to me on a wave of brandy and garlic.

"I just wanted to be sure everything was set to rights before I went to sleep. All is well, though, so good night, Father." I'd turned and tried to continue up the stairs when his heavy hand caught my arm.

"You should have a drink with me. It would be good for your hysteria."

I'd stopped moving the instant he'd touched me, afraid if I began to struggle away from him, he would only grasp all the tighter to my arm. "Father, I do not have hysteria. I only have weariness. The dinner party has tired me greatly and I need to sleep now."

Even on the dim landing I could see the intensity of his eyes as his hot gaze took in my loosened night robe and my free-falling hair. "Is that Alice's robe you're wearing?"

"No. This is my robe, Father."

"You did not wear one of your mother's dresses tonight." His hand had tightened on my arm, and I knew there would be bruised shadows there the next day.

"I refashioned one of Mother's dresses so that it fit me. That is probably why you didn't recognize it," I'd said quickly, sorry that I had been so stubborn—so vain—and that I had given him an excuse to focus his attention on me.

"Your figures are very similar, though." He'd lurched toward me, closing the space between us and making it thick with alcohol fumes and sweat.

Panic lent my voice strength and I spoke more sharply than I have ever heard any woman speak to him. "Similar, but not the same! I am your daughter. Not your wife. I bid you to remember that, Father."

He'd stopped moving toward me then and blinked, as if he couldn't quite focus on me. I used his hesitation to pull my arm from his loosened grasp.

"What is it you're saying?"

"I am saying good night, Father." Before he could grab me again I'd turned, lifted my skirts, and raced up the stairway, taking the steps two at a time. I did not stop running until I closed the door to my bedchamber and leaned against it. My breath had been short and my heart had been beating frantically. I was sure, quite sure, that I heard his heavy feet following me, and I'd stood, trembling, afraid to move, even after all sounds outside my room went quiet.

My panic finally subsided, and I'd gone to my bed, pulling the coverlet around me, trying to still my thoughts and find the calm within me again. My eyelids had just begun to flutter when there was a heavy footstep outside my room. I burrowed farther down within my bed linens and watched, wide-eyed, as the doorknob slowly, silently turned. The door opened a crack and I squeezed my eyes closed, held my breath, and imagined with all of my mind that I was back on my bend under the willow tree, safely cloaked in the comforting shadows.

I know he entered my room. I am sure of it. I could smell him. But I remained perfectly silent, not moving, imagining I was hidden completely in darkness. It seemed a very long time, but I heard my door reclose. I'd opened my eyes to find my room empty, though scented with brandy, sweat, and my fear. Hastily I'd gotten out of bed. Barefoot, I used all of my strength to push and drag my heavy chest of drawers in front of my door, barring the entrance.

And still I did not allow myself to sleep until dawn lightened the sky and I heard the servants begin to stir.

Sunday, I awoke and did what would become my morning ritual: I dragged the chest of drawers from before my door. Then I avoided Father the entire day. I told Mary that I was exhausted from the excitement of the dinner party, and that I wished to remain in my room, resting. I'd been quite firm, and Mary did not question me. She left me to myself, and for that I was grateful. I did sleep, but I also planned.

I am not mad. I am not hysterical. I do not know exactly what it is I see in my father's gaze, but I do know that it is an unhealthy obsession and it only reinforces my determination to leave Wheiler House soon.

I went to my looking glass, stepped out of my day dress, and studied my naked body, cataloging my attributes. I have high, firm breasts, a slim waist, and generous hips that have no inclination to fat. My hair is thick and falls almost to my waist. Like my mother's was, it is an unusual color—dark, but touched by rich auburn highlights. My lips are full. My eyes, again like Mother's, are undeniably striking. It is a true comparison to name them emerald in color.

With an utter lack of vanity or emotion I acknowledged that I was beautiful, even more beautiful than my mother, and she had often been called the most handsome woman in Second City. I also realized that, even though it was an abomination for his feelings to be such, it was my body, my beauty that my father so obviously coveted.

My mind and heart were still filled with Arthur Simpton, but they were also filled with a sense of desperation that frightened me. I needed Arthur to love me not only because he was handsome and kind and well positioned in the world. I needed Arthur to love me because he was my escape. Monday, I would visit his home. Staring into my looking glass I resolved to do anything to gain his vow and his troth.

If I am to save my life, I must make him mine.

Sunday evening, I'd expected Mary to bring me a dinner tray. Instead, Carson knocked on my door.

"Excuse me, Miss Wheiler. Your father requests that you join him for dinner."

"Please tell Father that I am still unwell," I'd said.

"Be pardon, Miss, but your father has had Cook make a healing stew. He said either you come to the dining room, or he will join you in your parlor here for dinner."

I'd felt a horrible sickness and had to clasp my hands together to keep from showing how I was trembling. "Very well, then. Tell Father I will join him for dinner."

With leaden feet I made my way to the dining room. Father was already seated at his place, with the Sunday paper open and a glass of red wine raised to his lips. He'd looked up as I entered the room.

"Ah, Emily! There you are. George!" he'd bellowed. "Pour Emily some of this excellent wine. That and Cook's stew will have her right as rain in no time—right as rain."

I sat without speaking. Father didn't seem to notice my silence.

"Now, you know, of course, that the opening of the Columbian Exposition is exactly one week from tomorrow, on May the first. After the success of your dinner party last night, Mrs. Ayer as well as Mrs. Burnham have taken an especial interest in you. The ladies have invited you to be included in their opening ceremony festivities, which will culminate in dinner at the University Club."

I gaped at him, not able to hide my surprise. The University Club was exclusive and opulent and not a place young, single girls were invited. Women were rarely allowed there at all, and those allowed were chaperoned by husbands.

"Well, have you nothing to say? Will you just gape like a codfish?"

I'd closed my mouth and lifted my chin. He wasn't drunk yet, and sober Father was much less frightening. "I am flattered by the ladies' attentions."

"Of course you are. You should be. Now, you must consider carefully what you will wear. First we will be going to the Midway, and then to the club. You should choose one of your mother's more elaborate gowns, but not one with such decadence that it would be out of place during the opening ceremonies."

One small thought had my heart lightening, and I'd nodded somberly. "Yes, Father. I agree the gown is very important. When I call on Mrs. Simpton tomorrow, I must ask her to help me in the choosing, and perhaps even in the alterations of it. She is a lady of impeccable taste and I'm sure she will—"

He'd waved his hand, cutting me off. "I have already had Carson send word to your mother's dressmaker to come to the house tomorrow. You have no time for such social frivolities as gallivanting about town. I have sent your excuses to the Simptons, and assured them it would *not* be necessary for that son of theirs to collect you. Instead, *I* will make a call on Mr. Simpton Monday evening for after-dinner brandy so that we may discuss business matters. That gout of his has kept him absent too long from board meetings. If Simpton will not go to the board, the president of the board will go to Simpton."

"What?" I'd pressed my fingers against my forehead, trying to stop the pounding in my temples. "You canceled my visit to the Simpton house? Why ever would you do that?"

Father's hard gaze met mine. "You have been ill all day, hiding away in your room. Too much excitement is obviously not good for your constitution, Emily. You will remain home this entire week so you will be fit for Monday next and the University Club."

"Father, I was simply tired from the party. Tomorrow I will be quite well. I am feeling more like myself already."

"Perhaps had you felt more like yourself earlier I would give credence to your words, but as it is, I have decided what is best for you—and that is saving yourself for Monday next. Have I made myself clear, Emily?"

I sent his hard gaze back at him, in my imagination filling it with the depth of my loathing. "Yes, you have made yourself clear." My voice had been stone.

Father's smile had been self-satisfied and cruel. "Good. Even your mother bowed to my will."

"Yes, Father, I know she did." I should have stopped there, but my anger allowed my words to be free. "But I am not my mother, nor would I ever desire to be."

"You could do no better in life than to be the Lady your mother was."

I'd let my voice mirror the coldness expanding within me. "Do you ever wonder, Father, what Mother would say if she could see us now?"

His eyes had narrowed. "Your mother is never far from my thoughts."

George began to serve the stew then, and Father neatly changed the subject, launching into a monologue about the ridiculous expenditures of the Exposition—like bringing an entire tribe of African pigmies to the Midway—and I sat silently, planning, thinking, plotting, and above all hating him.

I did not dare visit my garden that night. I excused myself before Father poured the brandy, smoothly using his own words against him by saying that I realized, after all, that he had been correct—I really was completely fatigued and must rest and be prepared for Monday next.

I dragged the heavy chest of drawers before the door, then sat atop it with my ear pressed against the cold wood, listening. Until well after moonrise I heard him pacing back and forth on his landing.

I was filled with frustration all of Monday. I so needed to call on Arthur and his parents! My only condolence was the fact that I was certain Arthur would see through Father's ruse. I had already warned him of Father's possessiveness. This would be but one more piece of evidence to prove my words true.

Surely the Simptons would at least attend the opening of the Columbian Exposition, if not the dinner at the University Club as well. I would see Arthur again Monday next—I must see Arthur again then. I would use all of my wits to find an opportunity to speak with him. It would be forward of me, but my circumstances were such that they demanded drastic actions. Arthur was kind and reasonable. He *and* his mother had paid me special interest. Surely, between the three of us we would find a way to get around Father's draconian behavior.

Draconian behavior. I had thought for many hours about how I could explain Father's unnatural possessiveness. I had learned from Camille's reaction when I had attempted, ever so slightly, to confide in her my distress about Father. Her shock had been complete and then she had excused my fears. Even Arthur, that night under the willow tree, had waved aside Father's behavior as that of a grieving widower who mourned the loss of his wife and was, therefore, understandably careful of his daughter. I knew better. I knew the truth. His increasing attentions to me were not simply overbearing and possessive, they were becoming horrifyingly inappropriate. It was an abomination, but I had come to suspect my father wanted me to take the place of my mother, *in all ways.* I had also come to believe that my suspicions could never be shared. So, instead of the truth I would paint a picture of a gruff, domineering father who frightened my delicate sensibilities. I would appeal to the gentleman within Arthur to rescue me.

It would be absurd for Father to turn down an honorable marriage proposal from a family with the wealth and social status of the Simptons. The alliance with their money and power would be too tempting. All I need do would be to secure Arthur's affections and convince him that my fear of Father's domination was so great that my health was at risk, and that we must have a short engagement. Father himself had taught me that men wanted to believe in the fragility and hysteria of women. Though Arthur was kind and good, he was a man.

The dressmaker arrived late Monday afternoon. It was decided that Mother's most elegant emerald silk gown would be reworked to fit my figure. I was still being fitted and pinned when Father had burst into my third-floor parlor without introduction or warning.

I could see the shock in the dressmaker's eyes. I had to raise my hands to cover my half-bared breasts as she had been in the process of repinning the dress's bodice.

Father's gaze had seared my body.

"The silk—an excellent choice." He'd nodded in approval as he'd paced a complete circle around me.

"Yes, sir. I agree. It will be lovely on your daughter," said the dressmaker, lowering her eyes.

"The gold lace is vulgar, though, for one so young as my Emily," Father had announced. "Remove it."

"I can do so, sir, but then the dress will be completely unadorned and, if you beg pardon for me saying so, sir, the occasion calls for something spectacular."

"I disagree." Father had stroked his beard and continued to study me and speak as if I weren't in the room, but only a soulless mani-kin. "Make the cut simple, but pleasing. The silk is the richest it was possible to acquire on this side of the world, and Emily's innocence is adornment enough for the dress. Otherwise, I will look to her late mother's jewels and, perhaps, find something appropriate for the evening."

"Very good, sir. It will be as you desire."

The dressmaker had been tucking and pinning, so she had not seen the heat in my father's eyes when he responded with, "Yes. It will, indeed, be as I desire."

I'd said nothing.

"Emily, I expect you to come down for dinner soon. Afterward, I will call on the Simptons so that you may go to your bed and rest. I want you in good health for Monday next."

"Yes, Father."

Except for one slight exchange, I had been silent during dinner. In the middle of Father's latest tirade about the excesses of the Exposition and his worry that he would, once again, be proved correct and the bank would lose money, he abruptly changed the subject.

"Emily, are you enjoying the time you volunteer with the GFWC each week?"

I am not sure what came over me. Perhaps it was how utterly exhausted I'd been by the subterfuge required to keep living a life wherein I had been forced to play the part of dutiful daughter to a man unworthy of the title of father. Perhaps it was because of the growing coldness within me, but I'd decided not to lie or evade Father's question. I met his gaze and told the truth.

"No. Mrs. Armour is a hypocritical old woman. The poor and homeless of Chicago stink and behave badly. Little wonder they have to live on the charity of others. No, Father. I do not enjoy volunteering at the GFWC. It is a charade and a waste of my time."

Humph! He'd made a noise through his nose followed by a guffaw of laughter. "You just spoke almost the exact words I used to your mother when she'd petitioned for the bank's charitable support of the GFWC. Well done you for understanding so quickly what your mother did not comprehend at more than two decades your senior."

I'd held my words. I would not barter my soul to be the ally of a monster. In silence I'd continued to push my food around my plate. Father had watched me while he drank deeply of the wine I had not had an opportunity to water.

"But contributing to a charity is of the utmost importance for those of our social and financial status. Let us imagine, for a moment, you could support a charity of your own inception. Tell me, Emily, what would that be?"

I'd hesitated enough to consider whether there could be any negative ramifications to answering him honestly, and I'd quickly decided I might as well speak my mind. It was obvious that I was his toy, his doll, his diversion. Nothing I said had the least bit of meaning to him at all.

"I would not support the lower stratus of humanity. I would uplift those who strive to reach beyond the bounds of the mundane. I have heard Mr. Ayer speak of his collection of fine Native art. I have heard Mr. Pullman discuss adding electricity to Central Station and his more exclusive cars. If it were within my power, I would create a Palace of Fine Arts, and perhaps even a Museum of Science and Industry, and I would nurture excellence rather than sloth."

"Ha!" Father had slapped the table so violently his wine had sloshed over the rim of his glass, and ran like blood into the fine linen tablecloth. "Well said! Well said! I am in complete agreement. I proclaim from here on you will no longer volunteer at the GFWC." Then he'd leaned forward and captured my gaze. "You know, Alice, we could accomplish great things together, the two of us."

My whole body had gone to ice. "Father, my name is Emily. Alice, your wife, my mother, is dead." Before he could respond I stood and, as George entered the room with the dessert, I'd pressed the back of my hand against my forehead and staggered, almost fainting.

"Miss, are you unwell?" The Negro had asked, frowning in concern.

"As Father said yesterday, I am still fatigued from Saturday night. Could you please call Mary so that she may escort me to my room?" I'd glanced at Father and added, "May I be excused, Father? I would not want my weakness to keep you from calling on the Simptons tonight."

"Very well. George, call for Mary. Emily, I expect your health to be better tomorrow."

"Yes, Father."

"Carson!" He'd bellowed, pushing away the dessert George had left for him. "Bring the carriage around at once!" Without another glance at me, he'd stalked from the room.

Mary had come in immediately thereafter, whispering about the fragility of my health and herding me to my bedchamber as if she were a hen and I her chick. I'd let her help me out of my day dress and into my nightgown, and then curled into bed, assuring her that

I would be well if I could just rest. She'd left me quickly, though I could see that she was honestly concerned for me.

What could I have told her? She'd seen the heat of Father's eyes on me. She and George and Carson, and probably even Cook, had to know that he stalked and imprisoned me. Yet none of them had said so much as one word against him. None of them had offered their aid in planning my escape.

No matter. I must be the vehicle of finding my salvation.

But that night, at least for an hour or two, I could orchestrate an escape, if only one of miniscule proportions.

Father would be gone to Simpton House, and would be ingratiating himself in the family and attempting to appear the concerned patriarch for his poor, frail daughter.

Again, no matter. It only meant that I could flee to my garden!

On silent feet I tiptoed down the broad stairway, around the foyer, and made my way out the servants' exit. I was not discovered. The house was as I preferred it, dark and quiet.

The April night was dark, as well. And I found a great ease in the concealing shadows. With no lights on in the rear of the house, and no moon risen as yet, it seemed as if the shadows had overtaken the walkway completely and, welcomingly, they caressed my feet. As I hurried to my willow, I imagined that I drew the shadows to me so that they cloaked my body in darkness so complete that it would never, ever, allow me to be discovered.

I'd followed the music of the fountain to my willow, parted the boughs, and gone to my bench, where I sat with my feet curled beneath me and my eyes closed, breathing deeply and evenly and searching for the serenity I'd always found there.

How long I was there I have no real recollection. I tried to keep time in mind. I knew I must leave my safe place well before Father might return, but I was drinking deeply of the night. I did not want to be parted from it.

The latch of the side gate to the garden had not been oiled, and its protesting voice had my head lifting from my hand and my body trembling.

Moments later a nearby twig on the garden path snapped and I was certain I could make out footsteps shuffling through the gravel of the walkway.

It could not be Father! I'd reminded myself. *He does not know I come to the garden!*

Or does he? Frantically, my mind had raced back to the conversations of Saturday night—the women complimenting me on my flower arrangements; Mrs. Elcott's sarcasm regarding my regard for the garden.

No. It had not been mentioned that I was spending time in the garden. No! Father could not know. Only Arthur knew. He'd been the only person who—

"Emily? Are you there? Please be there."

As if I'd conjured him, Arthur Simpton's sweet voice preceded him and he'd parted the boughs and stepped through the willow curtain.

"Arthur! Yes, I'm here!" Without allowing myself time to think, I'd acted on instinct and rushed to him, hurling myself into his surprised embrace, weeping and laughing at the same time.

"Emily, my God! Are you truly as unwell as your father says?" Arthur had held me away from him, studying me with concern.

"No, no, no! Oh, Arthur I am perfectly well now!" I hadn't stepped back into his embrace, his hesitance had warned me. *I must not appear too desperate—too forward.* So I'd wiped my face quickly and smoothed my hair, glad again of the concealing darkness. "Forgive me. I have embarrassed myself dreadfully." I'd turned away from him and hurried back to the safety of my bench.

"Think nothing of it. We both were surprised. There is nothing to forgive," he'd assured me in his calm, kind voice.

"Thank you, Arthur. Would you sit with me for a moment and tell me how you come to be here? I am so glad!" I'd not been able to stop myself from saying. "I've been so distraught at the thought of not visiting you and your family."

Arthur had sat beside me. "At this very moment your father is sipping my father's brandy and they are sharing cigars as well as banking stories. I come to be here because of my concern for you. Mother and I have both been dreadfully worried since receiving your Father's note yesterday saying that you were too unwell to pay any social visits at all this week. Actually, it was Mother's idea that I slip from the house and check on you tonight."

"Did you tell her about the garden?" My voice had gone sharp and cold with fear.

There was enough light for me to see that he was frowning. "No, of course not. I would not betray your confidence, Emily. Mother simply suggested that I call on you. And if you truly could not receive visitors I should leave a note of condolence with your maid. That is exactly what I have done."

"You spoke with Mary?"

"No, I believe it was your father's valet who answered the door."

I nodded impatiently. "Yes, Carson. What did he say?"

"I asked to be announced to you. He said you were indisposed. I said my parents and I were distressed to hear it, and asked that he give you our note of condolence tomorrow." He paused and his frown had begun to tilt up in the expression that had already become so beloved by me. "Then your father's man escorted me from the porch and watched me bicycle away down the street. When I was quite certain he was no longer watching, I circled back and entered through the gate as I did before, hoping that I might find you here."

"And so you have! Arthur, you are so clever!" I'd placed my hand over his and squeezed. He'd smiled and squeezed my hand in return. I released him slowly, understanding that I must not offer too much too soon.

"So you have recovered? You are well?"

I'd drawn a deep breath. I knew I must tread carefully. My future—my safety—my salvation depended upon it.

"Oh, Arthur, this is so difficult for me to tell you. It-it makes me feel disloyal to Father to admit the truth."

"You? Disloyal? I can hardly imagine it."

"But I'm afraid if I speak the truth I *will* sound disloyal," I'd said softly.

"Emily, I believe in truth. To tell it is to show a loyalty to God, and that is beyond any loyalty we hold to man. Besides, we are friends, and it is not disloyal to share a confidence with a friend."

"As my friend, would you hold my hand as I tell you? I feel so frightened and alone." I'd added a small, hiccupping sob.

"Of course, sweet Emily!" He'd captured my hand in his. I remember how wonderful it was to feel the strength and sureness of him, and what a stark contrast that was to Father's hot, heavy touch.

"Then this is the truth. It seems as if Father is going mad. He wishes to control my every move. I was not unwell after Saturday night, but he suddenly refused to allow me to call on your parents. He has also forbidden me to continue my volunteer work that I have been doing weekly at the GFWC, and that cause was so important to my mother!" I'd stifled another sob and clung to Arthur's hand. "He has said I may not leave Wheiler House until Monday next, and then I am only allowed to attend the opening of the Columbian

Exposition and the University Club dinner afterward because several influential ladies have requested my presence. I know it is as you said before, that Father is mourning the loss of his wife, but his behavior has become so controlling that it is frightening! Oh, Arthur, tonight at dinner when I tried to insist that I continue Mother's volunteerism with the GFWC I thought he was going to strike me!" I began to sob in earnest. Finally, Arthur pulled me into his arms.

"Emily, Emily, please don't cry," he'd said soothingly as he patted my back.

I'd pressed myself against him, crying softly on his shoulder, becoming increasingly aware that I had nothing on except my thin nightdress and my loosened dressing gown. I am not ashamed to admit that I thought of the beauty and fullness of my body as I clung to him.

His hand had stopped patting me, and had begun traveling up and down my back, warmly, intimately. When his breathing began to deepen and his touch had gone from consolation to caress, I'd realized his body had begun to react to the scant amount of cloth separating his hand and my naked flesh. I'd let instinct guide me. I'd held to him more tightly, shifting my breasts so that they were flattened against his chest, and then I pulled abruptly from his arms. With trembling hands I'd retied my dressing gown and turned away from him.

"What you must think of me! My behavior is so . . . so—" I'd stuttered, trying to find my mother's words. "So forward!"

"No, Emily. You must not think that, for I do not think that. You are obviously distraught and not yourself."

"But that is the trouble, Arthur. I *am* myself because I have only myself on which to depend. I am completely alone with Father. I so wish Mother was here and could help me." I hadn't had to pretend the sob that followed those words.

"But I am here! You are not alone. Emily, give me leave to speak to my mother and my father of your troubles. They are wise. They will know what to do."

I'd quelled a fluttering of hope and shook my head miserably. "No, there is nothing to be done. Arthur, Father frightens me dreadfully. If your father said anything to him about his treatment of me, it would only make my situation worse."

"Emily, I cannot promise that my father will not speak to yours. I had wanted more time to move ahead slowly and carefully, but with things as they are, it doesn't seem we are destined to be afforded time." He'd drawn a deep breath, and turned to face me on the bench. Gently, chastely, he'd taken my hands in his and continued. "Emily Wheiler, I would like to ask permission to formally court you, with the express purpose of making you my wife. Will you accept me?"

"Yes, Arthur! Oh, yes!" It hadn't just been relief at the escape that had opened before me that had me laughing and crying and hugging him tightly. I cared for Arthur Simpton, truly.

I might even love him.

He'd hugged me in return and then, laughing with me, drawn back, saying, "I have not stopped thinking of you from the moment I first saw you all those many months ago when you and your friend joined the Hermes Club. I think I have always known you would be mine."

I'd tilted my head back and looked up at him adoringly. "Arthur Simpton, you have made me the happiest girl in the world."

Slowly he'd bent and pressed his lips to mine. That first kiss had been an electrical shock to my body. I'd felt myself molding to his body and parted my lips invitingly. Arthur had deepened the kiss, tasting me hesitantly with his tongue. There had been no hesitation in my response. I'd opened to him, and even as I write this my body easily recalls the rush of warmth and wetness that his mouth had caused me to feel. Breathing deeply, he'd broken the kiss. His laugh had been tremulous.

"I-I must speak to your father soon. Tomorrow! I will call on him tomorrow."

My good sense had returned to me abruptly. "No, Arthur! You mustn't."

"But I don't understand. You are frightened, and time is of the essence."

I took his hand, pressed it to my breast, over my heart, and dared to say, "Do you trust me, my darling?"

His startled expression had softened instantly. "Of course I do!"

"Then please do as I say and all will be well. You must not speak to Father alone. He is not himself. He will not be reasonable. Arthur, he may even forbid you to see me, and then beat me when I protest."

"No, Emily! I will not allow that!

I'd breathed a sigh of relief. "I know how you can secure his blessing, my safety, and our happiness, but you must do as I tell you. I know Father far better than you do."

"Tell me what I must do to keep you safe."

"Be sure you and your parents attend the dinner at the University Club Monday next after the opening ceremonies on the Midway. At the dinner, in front of his peers and the great ladies of Chicago who have expressly requested that I accompany Father, *that* is when you must publicly ask permission to court me." Arthur had already been nodding in agreement, but I continued, "Even in his current unstable state, Father will not act irrationally in public."

"When I pledge my intentions, and my family supports me in my troth, your father will have no rational reason to refuse me."

I'd squeezed his hand more tightly. "That is true, but only if you do so in public."

"You are right, sweet Emily. Your father will have to act like himself then."

"Exactly! You are so wise, Arthur," was what I'd said. My thoughts, of course, had been much different.

"But will you be safe for a week? And how can I see you without provoking your father?"

My mind had whirred. "Father himself has said I am unwell. I will be a dutiful daughter and insist he is right, that my health is fragile and that I must rest, so as to be invigorated for Monday." And, I'd added silently, *I will go to my bed early and sleep with a heavy chest of drawers barring entrance to my chamber . . .*

Arthur had pulled his hand from me and gently tapped me on my nose. "And no more insisting that you volunteer at the GFWC. After we are married there will be years for you to follow your civic spirit, and volunteer as often and wherever you so desire."

"After we are married!" I'd said the words happily, mentally tossing away the rest of his sentence. "That sounds so wonderful!"

"Mother will be pleased," he'd said.

That had touched my heart and true tears had come to my eyes. "I'll have a mother again."

Arthur had embraced me, and this time I did not offer my lips to him. This time I'd only clung happily to him.

Too soon, he took his arms from around me. "Emily, I do not wish to leave you, but I am worried about the passing time. Father will not entertain long—his health will not allow it."

I was already standing before he'd finished speaking. Taking his arm I'd guided him to the edge of the shielding darkness of my willow. "You are absolutely right. You must leave before Father returns." And I had to rush to barricade myself within my bedchamber!

He'd turned to me. "Tell me how I can see you between now and next week. I must know that you are truly safe and well."

"Here—you may come here, but only at night. If it is safe, and if I am able to escape to the gardens I will pick a lily and place it in the latch of the garden gate. When you see the lily, you will know I'm waiting for you, my love."

He'd kissed me quickly and said, "Be safe, my dearest one." And then he'd hurried away into the darkness.

I'd been giddy with happiness and breathless with worry as I ran as swiftly and silently as possible back through the house and up the long flights of stairs. It had only been minutes after I'd pushed the chest of drawers before my door that, watching from within the curtains of my third-floor balcony, I saw Father stumble drunkenly from our carriage.

If he lurked outside my bedchamber, that night I did not know it. That night I slept soundly, door barricaded, content that my escape had been secured and that my future would be safe and happy.

Avoiding Father over the next week proved much easier than I'd anticipated, thanks to the financial travails of the Columbian Exposition. Father's bank was in turmoil regarding last-minute funding that Mr. Burnham was insisting the Exposition Committee approve.

Tuesday and Wednesday he'd rushed through dinner and then left immediately afterward, muttering darkly about architects and unrealistic expectations. Though he did not return home until well after moonrise, I did not escape to my garden. I did not pick a lily and chance being discovered. But on Thursday evening, when Carson announced that Father had come home only long enough to change into more formal attire and then depart for dinner and a board meeting at the University Club, I knew I would have hours of solitude before he returned.

I took dinner in my private parlor and dismissed Mary hours before usual, encouraging her to take the evening for herself and to visit her sister who lived across town in the meatpacking district. She had been grateful for the free time and, as I knew it would, word that the master and mistress of the Wheiler House were otherwise occupied spread through the servants. The house was silent as death before the sun had fully left the sky, and it had been ever so difficult for me to wait for true darkness and the concealing shadows of night. I'd paced and fretted until the moon, almost completely full, had lifted into the sky. Then I crept from my room, moving much more slowly than my heart had wanted my feet to go—but I understood I must be more careful now than ever. My freedom was in sight. Being discovered now, even were it only by one of our servants, could put everything I had worked so hard to orchestrate at risk.

Perhaps I should have remained in my room and trusted that Arthur would not forsake his word to me, but the truth was that I needed to see him. I longed to be touched by his kindness and his strength, and through his touch feel warmer, gentler emotions again. The tension within me had been building each day, and as Monday drew nearer and nearer, even though Father had largely been absent, I had begun to feel an increasing sense of foreboding. Monday should bring an end to my fear and suffering, but I could not shake the presentiment that something so terrible that even my imagination could not give it name, was waiting to happen to me.

Trying to put aside my foreboding and focus on the things I could control—the events I could understand—I'd dressed carefully, fully aware that I must draw Arthur to me and make him irretrievably my own. I'd chosen my finest chemise, a nightgown made of blush colored linen so soft that it felt like silk against my naked skin. From Mother's wardrobe I borrowed her finest dressing gown. It was, of course, made of velvet the exact color of our eyes. I'd stood before my looking glass as I wrapped it snuggly around my body, using the gold tasseled sash to belt it tightly so that the slimness of my waist contrasted beautifully with the generous curves of my bosom and my hips. But I'd been quite sure that the belted sash was tied in a bow, and one that could easily be loosened, as if on accident. I'd left my hair unadorned and free, combed it to a lustrous shine so that it tumbled in a thick auburn wave down my back.

I'd plucked a fragrant lily in full bloom from beside the garden path. Before I'd threaded it through the latch on the outward side of the gate I pulled one petal free and rubbed it behind my neck, between my bosoms, and on my wrists. Then, covered in the sweet scent of lily and the welcoming shadows of the night, I'd sat on my bench and waited.

Looking back I realize I couldn't have waited long. The moon, white and luminous, was still hanging low in the sky when I'd heard the garden gate squeak open and shoes crunch hurriedly on the gravel path.

I hadn't been able to sit calmly as I should have. I'd leaped up and on feet that did not seem to touch the spring grass, hurried to the edge of my willow curtain to meet my lover, my savior, my rescuer.

"Arthur!"

His arms were around me and his dear voice sounded like a symphony in my ears. "My sweet Emily! Are you well? Unharmed?"

"I am completely well now that you are here!" I'd laughed and tilted my face up, offering my lips to him. Arthur had kissed me then, and even pressed his body against mine, but as I'd begun to feel an increase in the tension of his body, he'd broken our embrace and, with a shaky laugh, bowed formally to me and offered me his arm.

"My lady, may I escort you to your seat?"

I'd swept my thick hair back and curtseyed, smiling teasingly up at him. "Oh, please do, kind sir. And, though I do not want to appear too forward, you should know that I have saved every dance tonight for you."

My words had made him laugh again, less nervously than before, and I did not cling too tightly to his arm, but gave him a chance to collect himself as he guided me to the bench. We sat, holding hands. I'd sighed happily when he, shyly, lifted my hand and kissed it gently.

"Tell me how you have been. There has not been one moment since last I saw you that you have not been on my mind," he'd said, sounding so earnest and young that he'd almost frightened me. How could anyone as good and kind as Arthur Simpton ever stand up to my father?

He wouldn't have to! I'd reminded myself as quickly as I do now. *Arthur only need make a public declaration for me—Father's fear of scandal and ridicule would do the rest.*

"I have been missing you," I'd said, holding tightly to his strong hand.

"But your father—he has not . . ."

When Arthur faltered and could not complete his question I continued for him, "Father has not often been at home for the past several nights. We have rarely spoken. I have kept to my chamber, and Father has kept to the business of financing the exposition."

Arthur had nodded in understanding. "Even my father has roused himself from his sickbed and has been dining and conducting business beside Mr. Pullman." He'd paused, and appeared uncomfortable.

"What is it?" I'd prodded.

"Mother and Father were completely pleased when I announced my intentions toward you. When I further explained your circumstances Mother, in particular, was concerned, especially after Father returned home Tuesday evening from a meeting and reported how very drunk your father had been, as well as impolite and belligerent, before the meeting had even come to a close."

I'd felt a thin ribbon of fear. "Oh, please, Arthur! Tell me your parents do not hold my father's excesses against me. It would break my heart if they did!"

"Of course not." He'd gently patted my hand. "To the contrary. Because Father witnessed Mr. Wheiler's behavior himself, he and Mother are even more determined that our courtship be short, our engagement formally announced, and you be rescued from such an undesirable situation as soon as is proper. If all goes as planned, this time next year you and I shall be wed, my sweet Emily!"

He'd pulled me gently into his arms then and hugged me. I'd been glad that I could bury my face in his chest because it had stopped me from screaming in impotent frustration. *One year! I could not stand to be in this abominable situation for another year!*

I'd slid closer to Arthur, secretly pulling at the sash which held Mother's dressing gown closed.

"Arthur, one year seems such a very long time from now," I'd murmured, lifting my face slightly, so that my breath was warm against his neck.

His arms had tightened around me. "I know. It seems long to me as well, but we must do things properly so as not to cause gossip."

"I'm just so afraid of what Father will do. He's drinking more and more, and when he is drunk he is frightening. Your father even said he was belligerent!"

"Yes, sweet Emily, yes," he'd said soothingly, stroking my hair. "But once we are betrothed, you will belong to me. Though it is impolite of me to say so, the truth is that my family has more social connections and is wealthier than yours. I want you to know that matters not at all to me, but it will matter to your father. He dare not offend my family, which means once we are engaged, he dare not offend—or harm—you."

Of course Arthur had spoken truthfully—or spoken as truthfully as he knew. The problem was that Arthur did not understand the depth of my father's depravity or the force of his desires.

But I could not enlighten him with such shocking information. All I could do was to be certain that Arthur Simpton was eager to marry me as quickly as possible.

So, I'd untangled myself from his embrace and stood with my back to him, my face in my hands, and sobbed softly.

"My Emily! My darling! What is it?"

I'd turned to face him, being sure that my movement caused my loosened dressing gown to open and expose the sheer chemise underneath. "Arthur, you are so good and so kind, I do not know how to make you understand."

"Simply tell me! You know we were friends before we were aught else."

I'd swept back my hair and wiped my cheeks, all the while watching how his honest gaze couldn't seem to help flickering downward to take in the curves of my body.

"I realize that your parents know what is best, and I want to do the right thing. I am just so afraid. And, Arthur, I must admit to you another secret."

"You may admit anything to me!"

"Each moment I spend away from you is an agony for me. It is forward and improper for me to admit it, but it is the truth."

"Come here, Emily. Sit beside me." I'd sat close to him and leaned against him. He'd encircled me with his arm. "It is not improper for you to admit your feelings for me. We are practically engaged. And I have already admitted that I spend every moment thinking of you. Would it ease your mind if I spoke to my parents and asked them to try to find an excuse to shorten our courtship period?"

"Oh, Arthur, yes! That would soothe my nerves ever so much!"

"Then consider it done. We will work this out together and someday soon you will know you have nothing more to fear from life except that your husband overindulges your every whim."

I'd rested my head on his shoulder and felt such a wonderful sense of well-being that the foreboding that had been shadowing me suddenly lifted, and I was finally, finally warm again.

I give my oath that I do not embellish, nor do I fantasize about what happened next. As we sat there together, within the shelter of my willow, the moon lifted high enough to send silver, illuminating light down on the fountain, lending the white bull and his maiden an otherworldly luster. The statues appeared to glow, almost as if the moonlight had breathed life into them.

"Isn't it beautiful?" I'd whispered reverently, feeling as if I was somehow in the presence of the divine.

"The moonlight is lovely," he'd said hesitantly. "But I must admit to you that your fountain is rather disturbing."

I'd been surprised. Still under the spell of the shining moon, I'd lifted my head so that I could look into his eyes. "Disturbing?" I'd shaken my head, not understanding. "But it is Zeus and Europa—

and it isn't my fountain. It was Mother's fountain. Father gifted her with it as a wedding present."

"I don't mean to criticize your father, but that seems an inappropriate gift for a young wife." Arthur's gaze had gone back to the moon-bathed fountain. "Emily, I know you are an innocent, and this is a subject better not discussed, but do you not realize Zeus rapes the maiden Europa after he, in bull form, steals her away?"

I'd tried to view the fountain with his eyes, but still all I saw was the strength and majesty of the bull, and the nubile beauty of the maiden. Then, for some reason, my voice spoke words that until then I had only considered silently.

"What if Europa went with Zeus willingly? What if she really loved him and he her, and it was only those who did not want them to be together—did not want them to have a happy ending—who called it rape?"

Arthur had chuckled and patted my arm patronizingly. "What a sweet romantic you are! I find I like your version of the myth better than the lewd one I know."

"Lewd? I have never considered it such." I'd stared at the fountain—Mother's fountain—now my fountain, and the warmth Arthur had made me feel began to cool.

"Of course you wouldn't. You know nothing of lewdness, my sweet Emily."

When he'd patted my shoulder again I'd had to force myself not to shrug away from his condescending touch.

"But speaking of fountains and gardens and such reminds me, my mother has begun supervising plans for extensive gardens on the grounds of Simpton House. She shared with me that she will be excited to have your input, especially as Simpton House will someday be your home."

I'd felt a jolt of unease then, though in retrospect it was foolish of me. In all the fantasizing and planning I'd done about my future and my escape, I'd not considered that I might be moving from one gilded cage to another.

"So, we will live with your parents, here in Chicago, after we are married?" I'd asked.

"Of course! Where else? I am sure we could not reside comfortably at Wheiler House, not with your father in such a disagreeable temperament."

"No, I would not want to live here," I'd assured him. "I suppose I thought you might consider returning to New York. Your father still has business interests there that need to be looked after, does he not?"

"Indeed he does, but my sisters' husbands are more than competent in that respect. No, Emily, I have no desire to leave Chicago. This city has my heart. It's ever changing. There is always something new happening here—always another excitement, a new discovery, rising with the dawn."

"I'm afraid I know little about that." I'd tried not to sound as cold and bitter as I felt. "For me, Chicago has shrunk to Wheiler House."

"There is nothing wrong with being an innocent, Emily. That is an intriguing form of excitement and discovery of its own."

He'd shocked me then by pulling me rather roughly into his arms and kissing me thoroughly. I'd allowed him the kiss, and a long, hot caress of my back when he slid his hand inside my loosened dressing gown. His touch had not repulsed me, but as I consider back I must admit, if only here in my silent journal, that I enjoyed his attentions much more when I initiated them. The urgency of his mouth had felt awkward and almost invasive.

I'd been the first to break the embrace, pulling away from him and modestly closing my dressing gown.

Arthur had cleared his throat and passed a shaking hand across his face before gently taking my hand in his again. "I did not mean to take advantage of our solitude and to press my attentions improperly."

I'd softened my voice and glanced shyly up at him from under my lashes. "Your passion did surprise me, Arthur."

"Of course it did. I'll show more care for your innocence in the future," he'd assured me. "You cannot know how very beautiful and desirable you are, though. Especially the way you are dressed."

I'd gasped and pressed my hands to my cheeks, though in the concealing darkness he could not see that his words had not made me blush. "I did not mean to be inappropriate! I didn't even consider my state of undress. I had to excuse my maid so that I could be sure not even the servants discovered that I was waiting for you."

"I don't blame you—not at all," he'd assured me.

"Thank you, Arthur. You are so good and kind," I'd said, though the words almost lodged in my throat. I'd made a show of yawning then, covering my mouth delicately with my hand.

"I forget how late it is. You must be exhausted. I should go, especially as it would not do to cross paths with your father—or at least not yet. Remember, I will ride by the garden gate each night between now and Monday, hoping to see a plucked lily."

"Arthur, please do not be angry with me if I cannot slip away. I will try my best, but I must be safe. You know how unpredictable Father has become."

"I could not be angry at you, my sweet Emily. But I will be hopeful. If it is at all possible, I pray I see you before Monday night."

I'd nodded and agreed heartily with him, and walked hand and hand with him to the edge of the willow curtain, where he'd kissed me softly and left, whistling to himself and stepping lightly, as if he hadn't a care in the world.

When I was sure he'd gone, I'd left my concealing willow and walked within the soothing shadows of the dark path to the house. No one stirred as I hurried to my bedchamber. There I pushed the chest of drawers before the door, and retrieved my journal from its hiding place.

Now, as I reread my words I do not believe I am doing Arthur or his family an injustice by encouraging his suit. I do care for him, and I will be a good and dutiful wife, but between now and Monday I will not pick a lily and place it on the garden gate. I will not tempt fate any more than I already must. Arthur will pledge himself to me on Monday night, in front of my father, his family, and our social peers. Father will not disgrace himself by refusing such a grand and glorious union of families. Then I only need to continue to prod Arthur into a hasty marriage, and all will be well.

It is Father and the abomination of his unnatural desires that make me cold. When I am free of Father, I will be free to love and live again.

I will not allow myself to believe anything else.

May 1st, 1893
Emily Wheiler's Journal

Tonight, Monday, May first, in the year 1893, my life has irrevocably changed. No, not simply my life, but my world. It seems to me as if I have died and been resurrected anew. Truly that analogy could not be more apt. Tonight my innocence was murdered, and my body, my past, my life, did die. Yet, like a phoenix, I have risen from the ashes of pain and despair and heartbreak. I soar!

I shall record the terrible, wonderful events in their entirety, even though I believe that I must end this recording and destroy this journal. I must leave no evidence. I must show no weakness. *I must be in complete control of this new life of mine.*

But for now the retelling of my story soothes me, almost as much as the concealing shadows of my garden, beneath my willow, once soothed me.

I already miss them, though. I cannot ever return to my garden and my faithful shadows, so this journal is all that is left to comfort me. And, comfort me it does. Though I have walked through the fires of Hell and looked its demons in the eyes, my hands do not shake. My words do not falter.

Let me begin when I awoke mid-morning on this fateful day. It was a wrenching cough that had me sitting up in bed, gasping for air. Mary came to me quickly, clucking with worry.

"Lass! I knew the look of ye yesterday boded ill. I can foretell a fever better than most. Let me summon the doctor," she'd said, plumping the pillows around me.

"No!" I'd coughed again, but tried to stifle it with my hand. "I cannot disappoint Father. If he believes I am truly ill, that I will not be able to accompany him tonight, he will be angry."

"But lass, ye cannot—"

"If I do not go with him he will attend the Exposition opening alone, as well as the dinner at the University Club. He will return home drunk and angry. You must know how terrible he can be. Don't make me say more, Mary."

Mary had bowed her head and sighed. "Aye, lass. I know he isn't himself when he's in his cups. And he has been countin' on your support today."

"The great Ladies of Chicago have demanded it," I'd reminded her.

She'd nodded somberly. "That they have. Well, then, there is only one thing to do. I'll make ye my grandma's herbal tea with lemon, honey, and a spoonful of Irish whiskey. As she used to say, if it doesna fix ye up, it will get ye through."

I'd smiled at her purposefully thickened accent and managed not to cough again until she'd left my bedchamber. I'd told myself her tea would help. After all, I couldn't be ill—I was never ill. I'd wondered if I had, over the past three days, spent too much time resting—and thereby avoiding Father as well as Arthur—and from feigning illness brought illness upon me.

No. That was a fantastical assumption. I was a bit unwell, probably from my frazzled nerves. The pressure of waiting and hiding and wondering could not be good for my constitution.

Mary had returned with her tea, and I drank liberally of it, allowing the whiskey to warm and soothe me. I believe it was then that time began to shift. Hours ran together. It had seemed I had only just opened my eyes when Mary was coaxing me into my green silk gown.

I remember sitting before the small mirror on my vanity and watching Mary dress my hair. I'd been mesmerized by the long strokes of her brush, and as she began to lift it into an elaborate chignon, I'd stopped her.

"No," I'd said. "Just pull it back from my face. Weave one of Mother's velvet ribbons through it, but leave my hair free."

"But, dove, that's a child's hairstyle, and not fit for a great Lady of society."

"I'm not a great Lady. I'm sixteen years old. I'm not a wife, or a mother. In this one respect, I would look my age."

"Very well, Miss Wheiler," she'd replied respectfully.

When she'd finished my simple coiffure, I'd stood and stepped before the full-length looking glass.

Regardless of what happened later that night, I will always remember Mary and the sadness that had filled her expression when she had stood behind me and the both of us took in my reflection. The emerald silk dress fitted me as if it had been poured over my body. It was perfectly unadorned by anything except the mounds of my breasts and the curves of my body. Almost none of my bare skin was revealed—the bodice was modest and the sleeves three quarters length—but the simplicity of the gown intensified the lushness of my figure. The only real concealment I had was my hair, though the thick fall of it was as sensual as the gown.

"You look lovely, dove," Mary had spoken quietly, and her mouth had formed a tight line as she'd studied me.

Fever and whiskey had flushed my face. My breath was shallow and it rattled in my chest. "Lovely," I'd repeated dreamily. "That is not how I would describe myself."

The door to my bedchamber had opened then and Father,

holding a square velvet jewelry box, had entered the room. He'd stopped abruptly and stared with us at my reflection.

"Leave us, Mary," he'd commanded.

Before she could move, I'd grabbed her wrist. "Mary cannot leave, Father. She is not finished helping me dress.

"Very well then." He strode to me. "Move aside, woman," he'd said, brushing Mary aside and taking her place behind me when she'd retreated to the corner of the room.

His eyes had burned my reflection. I'd had to force my hands to stay at my sides instead of instinctively attempting to cover myself.

"You are a picture, my dear. A picture." His gruff voice had the small hairs on my arms standing on end. "You know I've seen you so little this past week, I almost forgot how beautiful you are."

"I have not been well, Father," I'd said.

"You look well—well indeed! Your color is so high it makes me believe you have been looking forward to this evening as much as I."

"Nothing could make me miss this evening," I'd said coolly and truthfully.

He'd chuckled. "Well, my dear, I have something for you. I know you will wear them as proudly as your mother before you." He'd opened the square velvet box to reveal the triple strands of Mother's exquisite pearls. Taking them from the box, which he tossed away uncaringly, he lifted them and placed them around my neck, latching the thick, emerald studded clasp and then, with hot hands, he'd lifted my hair so that they settled heavily on my chest in a triple waterfall of luster.

My hand went up and touched them. They felt very cold against the heat of my skin.

"They become you, just as they did your mother." Father placed his hands heavily on my shoulders.

Our gazes had met in the mirror. I'd kept my revulsion carefully hidden, but when he just stood there and stared, I freed the rattling cough I'd been repressing. Covering my mouth, I stepped out of his grasp and hurried to my vanity where I finished coughing into a lace handkerchief before taking a long drink from Mary's tea.

"Are you truly ill?" he'd asked, looking more angry than concerned.

"No," I'd assured him. "It's just a tickle in my throat and my nerves, Father. Tonight is an important evening."

"Well, then, finish dressing and join me downstairs. The carriage is here and the opening of the World's Columbian Exposition waits for no man, or *woman*!" Chuckling at his poor joke, he left my room, banging the door against the wall after him.

"Mary, help me into my shoes," I'd said and coughed again.

"Emily, you really are not well. Perhaps you should stay home," she said as she bent to fasten the buckle on my beautiful silk and leather pumps.

"As with most of my life, I find that I have very little choice left to me. I must go, Mary. It will be all the worse for me if I stay."

She hadn't said anything more, but her pitying expression had been words enough.

I'd been grateful that the carriage ride to the Midway was blissfully short, though the roads were clogged with people. Even Father gaped around us. "My God! The entire world is in Chicago!" he'd exclaimed.

I was glad that he was too busy to stare at me, and too busy to notice that when I dabbed my lace handkerchief to my mouth it was because I was attempting to cover a cough.

Even ill and nervous as I was, I will never forget my first glimpse of the Midway and the miracle that was the World's Columbian Exposition. It was, indeed, a great, white city, luminous as my mother's pearls. Awestruck, I held to Father's arm and allowed him to lead me to the group of dignitaries that waited in an elegant group before the street entrance of the Midway Plaisance.

"Burnham! Well done—well done!" Father had bellowed as we joined them. "Ryerson, Ayer, Field! Look at the crowds. I knew if they could get it built it would do well, and by God, I was right," he'd blustered, then he'd freed my arm and hurried to join the other men.

As Father clapped Burnham on the back, Arthur Simpton stepped past him, met my eyes, and tipped his hat to me. His smile beamed happiness, and some of the tightness in my chest began to loosen as I returned his smile and even dared to mouth a quick "I have missed you so!" to him.

"Yes!" he'd shouted and nodded, and then had hastily rejoined the other men while my father was still engaged in an animated conversation with Mr. Burnham.

I'd joined the women's group, finding Mrs. Simpton easily, as she was so tall and handsome, though we hardly murmured the barest of polite hellos to one another. We were far too busy staring around us in wonder.

Mr. Burnham, who looked as if he had aged years since my dinner party, though it had only been little over a week ago, cleared his throat dramatically and then lifted an ivory and gold scepter with a miniature domed building atop it, and announced, "Friends, family, businessmen, and beloved ladies of Chicago, I bid you to enter the White City!"

Our group moved forward into pure fantasy. To either side of us was a living museum. As we walked down the Midway we passed groups of exotic village settings so that it appeared as if we had been transported instantly and magically from China to Germany, Morocco to Holland, and even to the darkest regions of Africa!

We didn't speak to each other more than to gasp and point from one marvel to another.

When we reached the Egyptian exhibit I was mesmerized. The

temple stretched above me, a golden pyramid, covered with exotic and mysterious symbols. I'd stood there, my breath coming rapidly, my handkerchief pressed against my lips stifling another cough, and the golden curtain that served as the door to the temple was pulled aside. A stunningly beautiful woman had emerged. She sat on a gilded throne that had been built atop two side-by-side poles that rested on the shoulders of six men, black as pitch and muscular as bulls.

She'd stood and commanded everyone's attention so completely that, even in the midst of the human cacophony surrounding us, fell a pocket of silence.

"I am Neferet! Queen of Little Egypt. I command that you attend me." Her voice was rich and distinctive, with an accent as seductive as it was foreign. She'd opened her golden cape, and shrugged it off to reveal a scant costume of silk and strands of golden beads and bells. From within the temple came a drum beat, sonorous and rhythmic. Neferet lifted her arms gracefully and began to undulate her hips in time with the music.

I had never seen a woman so beautiful or so bold. She did not smile. Truthfully, she seemed to mock the watching crowd with her icy gaze and her brazen looks. Her large dark eyes were painted heavily with black and gold. In the small indentation of her navel rested a sparkling red gemstone.

"Emily! There you are! Mother said she'd lost you. Our group has moved on. Your father would be very angry if he knew you had remained here, watching this lewd woman's show." I'd looked up to see Arthur frowning at me.

Staring around us, I realized he'd been right—his mother, the rest of the women, our entire group were all nowhere to be seen.

"Oh, I didn't realize I'd been left! Thank you for finding me, Arthur," I'd taken his arm, but as he led me away I'd glanced back at Neferet. Her dark gaze met mine, and very distinctly and haughtily, she'd laughed. I remember that at that moment all I could think was: *Neferet would never allow a man to lead her around—to order her about and tell her what to do!*

But I was not Neferet. I was queen of nothing, and I would rather be led around by Arthur Simpton than abused by my father. So I'd clung to Arthur, telling him how good it was to see him and how desperately I'd missed him, and listened to him talk on and on about how excited he and his parents were about our impending betrothal, and how he was not at all in the least bit nervous—though his torrent of words seemed to belie his protestations.

It was almost dusk by the time we found our group, finally rejoining them at the base of the enormous and fantastic creation Arthur explained they were calling a Ferris wheel.

"Emily, there you are!" Mrs. Simpton called to us and waved. I'd been mortified to see that she was standing beside Father. "Oh, Mr. Wheiler, did I not tell you my Arthur would find her safe and sound, and return her to us? And so he has."

"Emily, you must not wander off. Anything could happen to you out of my sight!" Father had gruffly taken me from Arthur's arm without so much as one word to Arthur or his mother. "Wait over there with the other women while I get our tickets for the Ferris wheel. It has been decided that we are all riding it before we depart for the University Club and dinner." He'd tossed me toward the group, and I'd stumbled into Camille and her mother.

"Excuse me," I'd said, righting myself. It had been then that I'd noticed what I hadn't earlier when the Midway had completely captivated my attention—Camille was with the women's group, as were several of my old friends: Elizabeth Ryerson, Nancy Field, Janet Palmer, and Eugenia Taylor. They seemed to form a solid and disapproving wall behind Camille and her mother.

Mrs. Elcott had looked down her long nose at me. "I see you're wearing your mother's pearls as well as one of her dresses, although the reworking of it has very much changed its appearance."

I'd already been more than aware of how the alteration of Mother's dress accentuated my body, and I could see by the censorious looks on their faces that while I had been distracted by the wonders of the fair, they had been judging and condemning me.

"And I see you are on the arm of Arthur Simpton," Camille added in a voice that echoed her mother's pinched tone.

"Yes, convenient of you to get yourself lost so that he had to find you," Elizabeth Ryerson had spoken up as well.

I'd squared my shoulders and lifted my chin. There was no point in attempting to explain my jewels or my clothes, and I certainly was not going to hide from these women, but I'd felt I must come to Arthur's defense. "Mr. Simpton was being a gentleman."

Mrs. Elcott had snorted. "As if you were being a lady! And it's *Mr. Simpton* now, is it? You appear to be much more familiar with him than that."

"Emily, are you quite well?" Mrs. Simpton had moved to stand beside me, facing the group of sour-faced girls. I noticed she was sending a hard look to Mrs. Elcott.

That had made me smile.

"Quite well, thanks to your son. Mrs. Elcott and Camille and a few of the girls were commenting on what a gentleman he is, and I was agreeing with them," I'd said.

"How nice of them to notice," Mrs. Simpton had said. "Ah, Emily, there are our men with the tickets." She'd pointed to Father, Mr. Elcott, and Arthur. The three of them were walking toward our group. "Emily, you will sit beside me, won't you? I have a dreadful fear of heights."

"Of course," I'd said. As Mrs. Simpton walked forward to meet her son, who was smiling distractingly at me, I'd felt Camille brush up close to me. Behind her I could feel the weight of the other girls' stares. Her whispered voice had been filled with spite. "I find that you are very changed, and not for the better."

Still smiling at Arthur I lowered my own voice, hoping that it would carry to Camille and the others behind her, and said with perfectly unemotional coldness, "I've become a woman and not a silly girl. As you and your friends are still silly girls, I can understand that you could not possibly find my changes are for the better."

"You have become a woman—one who doesn't care who she has to use or what she has to do to get what she wants," she'd whispered back. I heard murmurs of agreement from the other girls.

The coldness within me had expanded. What did this simpering child, or any of those other empty-headed, spoiled girls know of the changes I'd had to make to survive?

Without turning my smiling face from Arthur I said slowly, distinctly, and loudly enough for the entire spiteful group to hear me, "You are absolutely right, Camille. So it is best if you all stay out of my way. I would say that I would hate to see any of you hurt, but I would be lying, and I'd rather not do that."

Then I'd hurried to meet Father, who had been so overtaken by the anticipated trill of the Ferris wheel that he'd agreed to us sitting in the same cart box as the Simptons. As we soared two hundred and seventy-five feet in the air Arthur's mother held tightly to me with one hand, and her son with her other. She'd squeezed her eyes shut and trembled so violently her teeth had chattered.

I'd thought her a fool, though a kindhearted one. Her fear had made her miss the most spectacular view in the world. The blue waters of Lake Michigan stretched as far as one horizon, while before us was revealed an entire city that seemed to be built of white marble. As the sun sank behind the elegant structures, the powerful electric lights that surrounded the lagoon and the brilliant spotlight before the Electricity Building were turned on, making the Court of Honor and the sixty-five-foot-tall Statue of the Republic in the center of the lagoon blaze with magnificent white light that rivaled that of the fullest, brightest of moons. The light had been so bright, it had been quite uncomfortable for me to look at directly, though look I did.

Mrs. Simpton missed all of it, and her son missed quite a bit of the scenery, too, as he'd been so focused on soothing his mother's fear.

I'd vowed to myself that I would never, ever allow fear to make me miss magnificence.

Father insisted Mr. and Mrs. Burnham share our carriage to the University Club, which gave me a much needed and unexpected reprieve. Mrs. Burnham had been so excited by the Ferris wheel and the triumph of the electrical lighting, which only served to showcase her husband's talent, that I hadn't needed to engage in conversation with her at all. I'd simply appeared to mimic her expression as she'd listened attentively to her husband and Father blathering on and on about every miniscule detail of the fair's architecture.

Now that we weren't walking about, and my nerves had settled, I was finding it easier to control the terrible cough that had come so suddenly upon me. I was reluctant to admit it, even to myself, but I was feeling dreadfully weak and lightheaded—and there was a heat within my body that was becoming more and more uncomfortable. I believed I may truly be ill, and had been considering whether it would be wise for me to ask if Arthur could escort me home early. I must wait until after he declared his honorable intentions to Father, and Father accepted, but by the time the carriage reached the University Club, I was having a difficult time keeping my vision from blurring. Even the flickering gaslights in the club caused a tremendous pain to spike through my temples.

As I write this, I do so wish that I had understood the warning signs I was being given—my cough, my fever, my lightheaded sickness . . . and most of all, my aversion to light.

But how could I have known? As the night began I had been such an innocent about so many things.

My innocence would soon be irrevocably shattered.

We'd exited the carriages, and I'd been pleased to note that none of the other unmarried girls had been allowed to accompany their parents to the dinner. Their envious, condemning looks were, at least, an annoyance I didn't have to tolerate.

Our entire group arrived in a long line of carriages together and we had entered the ornate foyer of the University Club as one. I'd been relieved to notice that his father had joined Arthur and his mother. I'd only seen Arthur's father just a couple of times, and that was easily six or seven months ago when the family had first moved into their mansion not far from Wheiler House, but I was shocked to see how bloated and pale the old man looked. He leaned heavily on a cane and walked with a noticeable limp. I saw when Arthur and his mother caught sight of Father and me, and they steered Mr. Simpton our way.

Bloated and ill though he may be, Arthur's father had his same brilliant blue eyes as well as his charming smile. After he greeted Father and turned both on me, he said, "Miss Wheiler, it is a pleasure to see you again." I'd felt a great warmth for the old man and realized that though Arthur, too, may run to fat and poor health as he grew old, there would always be a spark left of the young man I'd married.

I'd curtseyed and returned his smile. "Mr. Simpton, I'm so glad you're feeling well enough to attend the dinner tonight."

"Young lady, the Grim Reaper himself could not have made me miss this evening," he'd said, eyes sparkling with our shared secret.

"Too bad you missed the Ferris wheel, Simpton. It was magnificent—simply magnificent!" Father had said.

"Magnificently terrifying!" Mrs. Simpton had exclaimed, fanning herself with her gloved hand.

I'd wanted to smile and perhaps say something clever to Mrs. Simpton about overcoming her fears, but a cough had caught me unaware, and I'd had to press the handkerchief against my lips and try to control my breathing. When the cough had finally spent itself and allowed me to breathe again, Father and the Simptons were all studying me with varying degrees of embarrassment and concern.

Thankfully, Mrs. Simpton's concern had voiced itself before Father's embarrassment. "Emily, perhaps you would accompany me to the ladies' lounge. I must splash some water on my face and collect my nerves before dinner, and while I'm doing that you could rest yourself on one of the settees."

"Thank you, Mrs. Simpton," I'd said gratefully, "I think I overexerted myself at the fair today."

"You must be careful of your health, Miss Wheiler," Mr. Simpton said kindly.

"Yes, I know. Father has been telling me the same thing recently."

"Indeed! Indeed! A woman's constitution is a fragile thing," Father added, nodding sagely.

"Oh, I couldn't agree more with you, Mr. Wheiler. Be certain I will take care of Emily." She'd turned to her husband then. "Franklin, do be a dear and be certain we are seated at the same table as

Mr. Wheiler and Emily so that the two of us will have an easy time finding the both of you when we join you for dinner."

"Of course, my dear," Mr. Simpton had said.

Arthur hadn't said one word, but his eyes had lingered on mine and he'd winked when Father hadn't been looking.

"Father, I'll be back soon," I'd said, and Arthur's mother and I had made a hasty escape.

Once in the lounge Mrs. Simpton drew me to a quiet corner. She pressed the back of her hand against my forehead. "I knew you would be warm! Your face is ever so flushed. How long have you had that cough?"

"Just since this morning," I'd assured her.

"Perhaps you should take your carriage home and rest. Arthur can choose another evening to speak to your father."

Panic had turned my stomach and I'd gripped her hands. "No, please no! It must be tonight. Father is getting worse and worse. Mrs. Simpton, look at me. Look at this gown."

Her eyes had flicked downward and then back to mine. "Yes, dear. I noticed it when first I saw you."

"Father forced the dressmaker to remake one of Mother's favorite gowns into this. I tried to reason with him, and tell him the style, the cut, were wholly inappropriate, but he would not listen. Mrs. Simpton, I pity Father and I know he is grieving for Mother even more than I am, but his grief is changing him. He must control everything about me."

"Yes, Arthur has told me he will not even allow you your volunteer work."

"Mrs. Simpton, Father won't allow me to leave the house at all unless he is with me. And his temper has become so frightening, so violent. I-I don't know how much longer I can bear it!" My shoulders had heaved and my body trembled as another coughing spell engulfed me.

"There, there. I can see that this is all very hard on your health. You are right. Arthur's intentions must be made public tonight, and soon tonight at that. Then I will escort you home myself so that you may rest and recover."

"Oh, thank you, Mrs. Simpton! You cannot know what this means to me," I'd sobbed.

"Wipe your eyes, Emily. You can show me how much this means to you by promising me that you will be a good and faithful wife to my son."

"I promise with all of my heart!" I'd meant the promise. I'd had no way of knowing that the rest of the night would alter everything.

Mr. Simpton had fulfilled his wife's request. He and Arthur were seated at the same table as Father and me, as well as Mr. and Mrs. Burnham, and Mr. and Mrs. Ryerson.

Father had gloweringly pushed a crystal flute filled with champagne the color of a blush over to me, saying, "Drink this. The bubbles may help your abominable croup!" I'd sipped it, folded my linen napkin onto my lap, and surreptitiously watched Arthur's mother whisper to him.

Arthur's face had gone pale, obviously with nerves, but he'd nodded tightly. He'd turned to his father, and I saw rather than heard him say, "It is time." Slowly, laboriously, his father had stood, raised his own champagne flute and, using a silver knife, tapped the crystal, silencing the crowd.

"Good ladies and gentlemen," he'd said. "I must begin by saluting Mr. Burnham and ask that you join me in a congratulatory toast to his genius, which was the driving force behind the World's Columbian Exposition."

"To Mr. Burnham!" the room roared.

"I am happy to announce that tonight's congratulations are not yet over. But I bow to my son, Arthur, as he must lead us in our next toast, and he has my blessing in doing so."

I'd felt my rapid heartbeat pounding in my chest as Arthur, tall, handsome, and somber-faced, stood. He'd walked around our table until he reached Father. He'd bowed first to him, and then he extended his hand to me. Though mine trembled terribly, I borrowed strength from him and stood by his side.

"What is the—" Father had begun to bluster, but Arthur neatly cut him off.

"Barrett Wheiler, I publicly, formally, and with the blessing of my family, declare my deepest affections for your daughter, Emily, and ask your permission to court her with the express and honorable purpose of marriage." Arthur's voice was deep and did not falter one bit. It carried throughout the opulent dining hall.

In that moment I can truly say that I loved him utterly and completely.

"Oh, well done, Simpton! Congratulations indeed!" It was Mr. Burnham, and not my father who stood. "To Emily and Arthur!" The room echoed his toast, and then there was an eruption of cheers and well wishes. As Mrs. Ryerson and Mrs. Burnham gave me soft kisses and made over Arthur and me, I saw Arthur's father limp over to my father. I held my breath. Though Father's expression was dark, the two of them shook hands.

"It is done." Arthur had been watching as well, and he whispered the words to me as he bent and kissed my hand.

I don't know whether it was with relief or with illness, but it was then that I fainted.

When my senses returned there was pandemonium around me. Father was bellowing for a doctor. Arthur had lifted me and was carrying me from the room into the sitting area outside the great hall. Mrs. Simpton was trying to reassure Father and Arthur that I was simply overexcited and had not been feeling well all day.

"And the poor thing's gown is entirely too tight," she'd said as Arthur placed me gently on a settee.

I'd tried to reassure Arthur and agree with his mother, but I could not speak through the cough that gripped me. Next I knew there was a gray bearded man bending over me, feeling my pulse, and listening to my chest with a stethoscope.

"Definitely not well. Fever . . . rapid pulse . . . cough. But in light of the events of the evening, I'd say all except the cough could be attributed to woman's hysteria. Rest quiet, and perhaps a hot toddy or two are what I prescribe."

"So, she will be well?" Arthur had taken my hand.

I'd managed to smile at him and answer for myself. "Quite well, I promise. All I need is rest."

"She needs to get home and to her bed," Father had said. "I shall call our carriage and—"

"Oh, Father, no!" I'd forced myself to smile at him and sit up. "I would not rest well knowing I had been the cause that took you from this special dinner you have so looked forward to."

"Mr. Wheiler, please allow me the honor of escorting your daughter home." Mr. Simpton surprised me by speaking up. "I understand what a burden it is on the family when one member is not well, as I have not felt completely myself for months. This evening I agree with little Emily—rest shall do us both a world of good—and that should not hinder the celebration for the rest of you. Mr. Wheiler, Arthur, please stay. Eat, drink, and make merry for Emily and for me."

I'd covered my smile with a cough. Mr. Simpton had put Father in a position twice in one night wherein he would look ridiculous if he refused him. Had I not felt so terribly ill I would have wanted to dance about with joy.

"Well, indeed. I will allow you to see my Emily home." Father's voice had been gruff, verging on impolite, but everyone around us acted as if they did not notice.

Everyone, that is, except Arthur. He'd taken my hand and met Father's dark gaze, saying, "*Our* Emily now, Mr. Wheiler."

It had been Arthur and not Father who had helped me to the Simpton carriage, and Arthur who had kissed my hand and had bidden me a good night, saying that he would call on me the next afternoon.

Father had stood alone, glowering, as the lovely, well-upholstered carriage had driven away with Mr. Simpton and me smiling and waving.

It had seemed that I was a princess who had finally found her prince.

Wheiler House was unusually still and dark when the Simpton carriage left me on the walkway to the front door. Mr. Simpton had wanted to see me inside, but I had protested that he not inflame his leg any more than necessary, and explained that Father's valet, as well as my maid, would be waiting within.

Then I'd done something that had surprised myself. I'd leaned down and kissed the old man's cheek.

"Thank you, sir. I owe you my gratitude. Tonight you saved me—twice."

"Oh, not at all! I'm pleased by Arthur's choice. Get well, child. We will talk again soon."

I'd been thinking how fortunate I was to have found Arthur and his affable parents when I entered our foyer and lit the gaslight within. After the soothing darkness of the carriage and the night, the light seemed to send spikes through my temples and I snuffed it out immediately.

"Mary!" I'd called. The house didn't stir. "Carson! Hello!" I called again, but my words dissolved within a terrible cough.

I'd longed for the comforting shadows of my garden and the concealing darkness beneath my willow—how I believed it would have soothed me! But I was feeling so very ill that I knew I must get abed. Truth be told, the severity of my cough and the burning of my fever was beginning to frighten me. I struggled up the three flights of stairs, wishing Mary would hear me and appear to help me.

I was still alone when I made it to my bedchamber, pulled the cord that would ring the summoning bell in Mary's small, basement room, and collapsed on my bed. I have no idea how long I lay there, struggling to breathe. It seemed a very long time. I'd felt like sobbing. Where was Mary? Why had I been left alone? I'd tried to unhook the tight little buttons that ran from the back of my neck all the way down to my waist and to take off the green silk gown that was so restrictive, but even feeling completely well that would have been nearly impossible. That night I hadn't even been able to manage unclasping Mother's pearls.

Fully dressed, I lay on my bed, gasping for breath between coughs, in a state that was more dreamlike than awake. A wave of weakness washed through me, closing my eyes. I believe I might have slept then because when next my senses registered the world around me, I thought I was in the grip of a hideous nightmare.

I'd smelled him before I'd been able to open my eyes. The scent of brandy, sour breath, sweat, and cigars filled my bedchamber.

I'd forced my eyes open. He had been a hulking shadow over my bed.

"Mary?" I'd spoken her name because I hadn't wanted to believe what my senses told me.

"Awake, are you?" Father's voice was thick with alcohol and anger. "Good. You need to be. We have things to settle between us."

"Father, I am ill. Let's wait and talk tomorrow when I am better." I'd pushed myself farther back against my bed pillows, trying to put more space between us.

"Wait? I've waited long enough!"

"Father, I need to call Mary. As the doctor said, she must make me a hot toddy so that I can rest."

"Call Mary all you like—she won't come. Neither will Carson or Cook. I sent them all to the fair. Told them to take the whole night off. There is no one here except the two of us."

That's when I became afraid. Summoning all the strength I could, I slid to the other side of the bed, away from him, and stood. Father was old and drunk. I was young and fleet footed. If I could just slip around him, he would not be able to catch me.

But that night I had not been a fleet-footed girl. I had been dizzy with fever and weak with a cough that would not let me catch my breath. As I'd tried to dart around him, my legs had felt as if they were made of stone and I'd stumbled.

"Not this time. This time we settle it!" Father grabbed my wrist and pulled me back.

"We have nothing to settle! I am going to marry Arthur Simpton and have a good and happy life away from you and your perversions! Do you think I don't know how you look at me?" I'd shouted at him. "You disgust me!"

"I disgust you? You whore! You are the one who tempts me. I see how you watch me—how you flaunt yourself to me. I know your true nature, and by the end of this night you will know it, too!" he'd roared, sending spittle flying into my face.

He struck me then. Not on my face. Not once that night did he strike my face. One of his hot hands held both my wrists together in a viselike grip, pulling my arms over my head, while his other hand, curled into a fist, battered my body.

I'd fought him with all my might. But the more I fought, the harder he beat me. I had been propelled by terror, like a feral creature cornered by a huntsman, until he grasped the front of my silk dress and ripped it downward, tearing Mother's pearls with the delicate fabric so that they rained around us as my breasts were fully exposed.

My body betrayed me then. It could no longer fight. I went cold and limp. When, with an animalistic growl, he'd pinned me on my bed, lifted my skirts, and rammed himself within the most intimate part of me as he bit and groped my breasts, I'd not moved. I'd only screamed and screamed until my throat had gone raw and my voice was lost.

It had not taken him long to finish. Once spent he'd collapsed, his great, sweating weight pressing me down.

I'd thought I would die, bleeding and broken beneath him, and smothered by pain and loss and despair.

I had been wrong.

He'd begun to snore, great snorting breaths, and I realized he was fully asleep. I dared to prod his shoulder and, with a grunt, he'd rolled off me.

I hadn't moved. I'd waited until his snoring resumed. Only then did I begin inching away. I'd had to stop frequently and press my hand against my lips to contain the wet coughs, but finally I was free of the bed.

The numbness of my body was gone, though I'd wished mightily that it would return. But I did not allow the pain to make me hesitate. I moved as quickly as my battered body would allow and pulled my cloak from the armoire. Then slowly, quietly, I gathered up the loose pearls, as well as the emerald clasp, and secreted them, and this, my journal, within the deep pockets of the cloak.

I left through the rear door. Though I couldn't chance pausing beneath my willow, I walked my dark path one last time, calling the concealing shadows to me and drawing comfort from the familiar darkness. When I reached the garden gate, I paused and looked back. The full moon had illuminated the fountain again. Europa's marble face was turned toward me and through my blurred vision it seemed as if the water from the fountain had turned to tears, washing her cheeks as she wept for my loss. My gaze went from the fountain to my pathway and I realized that behind me I had left a trail of blood.

I went out the garden gate that had allowed Arthur, and what I believed to be salvation, into my life. I would retrace Arthur's steps. He would still be my salvation—he must still be my salvation.

The Simpton Mansion was not far down South Prairie Avenue. I'd been grateful for the lateness of the hour. I met very few people as I stumbled along the walkway, enveloped in the cloak I clutched tightly about me.

You might think that during that painful journey I would have been imagining what I should say to Arthur. I had not. My mind hadn't seemed my own, just as, earlier, my body had stopped obeying me. My only thoughts were that I must keep moving forward, toward safety, kindness, and Arthur.

It had been Arthur who found me. I'd paused in front of the Simpton Mansion, leaning on the cold wrought-iron fence that decorated the boundary around it. I'd been trying to catch my breath and to order my thoughts into finding the latch to the gate, and Arthur, leading his bicycle, had burst from the very gate I had been approaching.

He'd seen me, and paused, in the darkness not recognizing my cloaked and hooded form.

"May I help you?" His voice, kind and familiar, had broken me.

I'd shrugged off the hood and, in a voice so damaged I barely recognized it as my own, I cried, "Arthur! It's me! Help me!" Then a coughing seizure, more severe than all the rest, took my body over and I began to crumble to the ground.

"Oh, God! Emily!" He'd thrown his bicycle aside and caught me in his arms as I fell. My cloak had opened then, and he'd gasped in horror at the sight of my torn dress, and my broken and bloody body. "What has happened to you?"

"Father," I sobbed, trying desperately to speak as I struggled to breathe. "He attacked me!"

"No! How could this be?" I watched his gaze go from my untouched face down to the wounds on my exposed breasts, and to my ripped skirt and my blood-coated thighs. "He—he has completely abused you!"

I'd been staring into his blue eyes, waiting for him to comfort me and take me within to his family where I could be healed and where Father would, eventually, be made to pay for what he had done.

But instead of love or compassion or even kindness, I saw shock and horror in his eyes.

I'd shifted my body, covering myself with my cloak. Arthur made no move to keep me in his arms.

"Emily," he'd begun, in a voice that sounded strange, and stilted. "It is clear that you have been violated, and I—"

I will never know what Arthur was going to say because at that moment a tall, elegant figure stepped from the shadows and pointed a long, pale finger at me, saying, "Emily Wheiler! Night has Chosen thee; thy death will be thy birth! Night calls to thee; hearken to Her sweet voice. Your destiny awaits you at the House of Night!"

My forehead exploded in blinding pain and I covered my head with my hands, as I trembled violently and waited to die.

Remarkably, with the next breath I drew, my chest loosened and sweet air flowed freely within me. I opened my eyes to see that Arthur was standing several feet from where I'd crouched, as if he'd begun to run away. The dark figure was a tall man. The first thing I noticed about him was that he had a sapphire-colored tattoo on his face that was made of bold lines spiraling from the crescent moon in the center of his forehead, across his brow and down his cheeks.

"My God! You're a vampyre!" Arthur had blurted.

"Yes," he'd answered Arthur, but had barely spared him a glance. All of his attention was focused on me. "Emily, do you understand what has happened to you?" the vampyre asked me.

"My father has beaten and raped me." As I spoke the words, clearly and plainly, I felt the last of the sickness leave my body.

"And the Goddess, Nyx, has Marked you as her own. Tonight you leave the life of humans behind. From here on you answer only to our Goddess, our High Council, and to your own conscience."

I'd shaken my head, not truly understanding. "But, Arthur and I—"

"Emily, I wish you well, but this is all too much for me. I cannot, will not, have such things in my life." And Arthur Simpton had turned and fled back to his parents' house.

The vampyre moved to me and with grace and preternatural strength, he lifted me in his arms and said, "Leave him and the pain of your old life behind you, Emily. There is healing and acceptance waiting for you at the House of Night."

That is how I came to finish the record of what happened to me this horrible, wonderful night. The vampyre carried me to a black carriage, drawn by four perfectly matched black mares. The seats inside were black velvet. There were no lights at all, and I welcomed the darkness, finding comfort in it.

The carriage took us to a palace made truly of marble, and not the weak pretence of stone that the humans of Chicago had created for their fair.

As we drove through the gate in the thick, high walls, a woman met me on the front stairs. She, too, had a sapphire crescent tattoo in the middle of her forehead, and markings surrounding it. She waved joyously, but when the carriage stopped and the vampyre Tracker had to lift me from within, she hurried to me. She shared a long look with the other vampyre before turning her mesmerizing gaze on me. She touched my face gently and said, "Emily, I am your mentor, Cordelia. You are safe here. No man will ever harm you again."

Then she took me to a sumptuous private infirmary, bathed and bandaged my body, and bade me to drink wine laced with something warm and metallic tasting.

I still sip on the dark drink as I write. My body aches, but my mind is my own again. And I find, as always, I am learning . . .

May 8th, 1893
~~*Emily Wheiler's Journal*~~
Neferet's Journal
Entry the first and last

I have decided. I have made my choice. This will be my last journal entry. In my retelling of the end of Emily Wheiler's story and the beginning of Neferet's wondrous new life, I complete what I began here in these pages six months ago.

I am not mad.

The horrible events that befell me and that are recorded in these pages did not happen because of hysteria or paranoia.

The horrible events that befell me happened because, as a young human girl, I had no control over my own life. Envious women condemned me. A weak man rejected me. A monster abused me. All because I lacked the power to affect my own fate.

Whatever this new life as a fledgling and, I can only hope, a fully Changed vampyre brings me, I make one promise to myself: I will never allow anyone to gain control over me again. No matter the cost—I will choose my own fate.

That is why last night I killed him. He used and abused me. When he did that he had full control over me. I had to kill him to regain that control. No one will ever harm me without suffering equal or more in return. I pretend to Cordelia and the School Council that I hadn't intended to kill him, that he had forced me into it, but that is not the truth. Here in these final pages of my journal, I will tell only the truth.

And then the truth will be buried with this book, and with it I bury my past.

Even my mentor, Cordelia, a High Priestess who has power and beauty in equal measure, and who has been in the service of the Goddess of Night, Nyx, for almost two centuries, does not understand my need to balance the scales of my life. The night after I'd been Marked and entered the House of Night, I'd left the infirmary and she'd shown me to my new bedchamber—a beautiful, spacious room that, because of my wounded body, I had to myself. There she tried to talk with me about him.

"Emily, what that man did to you was abominable. I want you to listen closely to me. You are in no way to blame for the violence he did to you," she'd said.

"I don't believe that's how he and his friends would see it," I'd said.

"Human law and vampyre law are not one in the same. Humans have no jurisdiction over us."

"Why?" I'd asked.

"Because humans and vampyres are not the same. There are, indeed, more of them than us, but we few hold greater wealth and power as individuals than they can ever hope to attain. We are stronger, smarter, more talented, and more beautiful. Without vampyres, their world would be nothing more than a snuffed candle."

"But, what if he comes after me?"

"He will be stopped. That man will never harm you again. You have my oath on that." Cordelia hadn't raised her voice, but I could feel the power of the anger in her words brush across my skin, and I believed her.

"But what if I want to go after him?"

"To what end?"

"To make him pay for what he did to me!"

Cordelia had sighed. "Emily, we cannot imprison him any more than he can apprehend one of us."

"I don't want him imprisoned!" I'd shouted.

"What is it you want?"

I'd almost admitted the truth to her, but there was something about her serene gaze and the honesty in her beautiful face that stayed my words. I hadn't made my choice yet, but instinct told me to keep my deepest thoughts and desires to myself, and that is exactly what I did.

"I want him to admit he is a monster, and that what he did to me was wrong," I'd said instead.

"And you think that would help you heal?"

"Yes."

"Emily, I tell you truly that I believe you have a unique power waiting to form within you. I sensed it when first I saw you. I feel that our Goddess has great gifts prepared for you. You could be a major force for good, especially as you have been wounded so viciously by evil, but you must choose to heal and to release the evil done to you, to let it die with your old life."

"So he will never pay for what he did to me." I hadn't framed the words as a question, but she'd answered.

"Perhaps not in this lifetime. That is no longer your concern. Daughter, one thing I have learned during the past two centuries is that the need for retribution is a curse, because it is impossible to attain. No two people, human or vampyre, will ever love, hate, suffer, or forgive in the same way. So, an insatiable need for retribution and vengeance becomes a poison that will taint your life and destroy your soul." She'd touched my arm and continued more gently. "It may help if you follow the tradition of countless fledglings before you and choose a new name to symbolize your new life."

"I will consider it," I'd said. "And I will also try to forget him."

I didn't have to consider long. I knew what name I wanted to carry into my new life.

I have tried to forget him. When I look in the mirror and see the bruises that purple my white flesh, I remember him. When I ache and bleed from the most private parts of my body, I remember him. When I wake screaming, my voice hoarse from reliving the nightmare of what he did to me, I remember him.

So he had to die. If I am to be cursed by my need for retribution and vengeance, then so be it.

I waited one week. It took that long for my body to recover. And recover, I did. I had been Marked for only seven days, yet already I was stronger than a human female. My fingernails had hardened and lengthened. My hair was thicker, fuller, longer than before. Even my emerald eyes were beginning to change.

I overheard one of the Sons of Erebus, the Warriors whose sole duty it was to protect fledglings and female vampyres, say that my eyes were becoming the most fascinating emeralds he'd ever gazed upon.

I liked what I was becoming, which made me even more determined to rid myself of my past.

It hadn't been difficult to leave the House of Night. I was not a prisoner. I was a student, respected and appreciated for my beauty and for what Cordelia called my potential. As students we had access to a fleet of carriages and more bicycles than were owned by the entire membership of the Hermes Club. We could leave the campus whenever we wished. I was afforded almost unlimited freedom. The only caveat was that we use a makeup paste to cover the outlined crescent moons in the center of our foreheads, and to dress modestly as to draw as little attention to ourselves as possible.

My dress had been modest. Though it was elegantly made of fine linen, it was dove gray in color, high-necked, and unadorned. Without touching me, one would not know how expensive it was—and no one was going to be allowed to touch me.

My hooded cloak easily concealed the only immodest part of my ensemble—Alice Wheiler's pearls. My choice to restrand and wear them that night had been premeditated. The idea to do so had come to me as I sat in my new garden and waited for my body to repair itself.

The House of Night is a school, but it is an unusual one. Classes are held only at night. Students and our professors and mentors, priestesses and warriors, sleep during the day, safe behind thick marble walls, which have been heavily enforced with an otherworldly magick that draws strength from the night, the moon, and the goddess who reigns over us all.

Cordelia had explained to me that I would be excused from classes until my body was fully healed, but then I would join the other fledglings and be immersed in a fascinating curriculum, which would grow and continue over the next four years, culminating in one of two things: my Change to full vampyre or my death.

The only death that concerned me was his.

As I gained strength and wellness, I explored the palatial House of Night and the grounds that were encircled by a white marble wall. I'd thought the gardens of Wheiler House beautiful, and though I would never forget my willow, my fountain, and the comfort I found within the shadows there, after seeing the vampyres' gardens all others would pale in comparison.

The House of Night gardens had been created to be fully enjoyed only after the sun set. Night blooming jasmine, moon flowers, evening primrose, and lilies opened to the moon and released a fragrance that was sweet and satisfying, and stretched on for acres and acres. Dozens of fountains and statuary were situated throughout the grounds, each of them illustrating a different version of the Goddess, Nyx.

I'd searched and easily found a willow tree that curtained an area not far from a particularly beautiful marble statue of the Goddess, arms raised, lush body unashamedly naked. Under my new willow, I also found the familiar darkness and the shadows that soothed my battered body and spirit.

It was there that I sat, cross-legged on a carpet of moss, and poured the pearls from Alice Wheiler's broken necklace onto a dark cloth. Then, surrounded by concealing, comforting shadows, I took a wire, thin as a hair, and built a new necklace from the remains of the old one. This one was not to be triple-stranded and elegant. This one was going to be one long circle of pearls—very much like a noose.

Cordelia had been confused when I'd asked for the wire, the stringing needle, the crimpers and scissors. When I explained I wanted to make my old mother's necklace anew, just as I was making my life anew, she had given me the supplies I needed, but I could tell by her countenance that she did not approve.

I didn't need her approval.

The night I finished the necklace, I had been cutting the wire to crimp around the emerald clasp and I'd pricked my finger with the raw, sharp edge of the wire. I'd watched, fascinated, as my blood had followed the slim thread to disappear within the pearls. It had seemed right that my blood had sealed the remaking of the necklace.

The long, single strand had been a comforting weight against my bosom as I left the House of Night and began the three-mile walk to South Prairie Avenue. The waning moon was high in the sky, but shielded by clouds it afforded little light. I'd been glad of the cloud cover. I'd felt comforted by the darkness and as one with the shadows, so much so that by the time I reached the Wheiler House it seemed as if I had become a shadow myself.

It was well past midnight when I unlatched the garden gate and, moving in silence, retraced the path that just one week ago I had left splattered with my blood.

The servants' entrance was, as usual, unbarred.

The house slept. Except for two gaslights at the base of the staircase, it was dark. I snuffed the lights as I reached the stairs. In shadow, I moved up one landing and another. I felt as if I floated with the darkness.

His door was unbarred. The only light in his room came from the cloud-shrouded moon shining through his long beveled windows.

It was light enough for me.

His room stank of him. The noxious scent of alcohol and sweat and foulness had my lip curling, but it didn't deter me.

Silently, I moved to his bedside and stood over him, just as he had stood over me one week ago.

I lifted the pearls from around my neck and held them, taut and ready in my hands.

Then I gathered phlegm in my mouth and spit in his face.

He woke, blinking in confusion, and wiping my spittle from his face.

"Awake, are you? Good. You need to be. We have things to settle between us." I'd repeated his words to him.

He'd shaken his head, as if coming inside from a rainstorm. Then, his eyes opened wide in shocked recognition. "Emily! It is you! I knew you'd come back to me. I knew what that Simpton boy had said about a vampyre Marking you and taking you away had been a lie."

As he struggled to sit up I struck. With speed and strength no human girl could have commanded, I wrapped the pearls stranded on wire around his fat throat. Then I closed the noose. As I squeezed and squeezed I locked my gaze with his and in a voice that held no hint of human softness I spoke.

"I didn't come back *to* you. I came back *for* you." His body began to convulse and his thick, hot hands beat against me, but I was no longer a sick, weak girl. His blows marked me, but they did not stop me. "Yes, hit me! Bruise me! That will only give evidence to my story. You see, I had to defend myself when you attacked me again. I'd only wanted you to admit what you did to me was wrong, but you tried to violate me again. This time you failed."

His eyes had bulged in his scarlet face until it looked as if he wept tears of blood. Just before he choked on his last breath I told him, "And I am not Emily. I am Neferet."

Afterward, I unwrapped the pearls from around his neck. They had cut deeply into his flaccid flesh and were covered in his blood. I carried them carefully as I retraced my path through the dark streets of Chicago. When I reached the metal State Street Bridge, which spanned the fetid depths of the Chicago River, I paused and dropped the necklace into the water. It seemed that it floated on the dark water for quite a long time and then black, oily tendrils lapped over it, pulling the pearls under the surface like a sacrifice accepted.

"That ends it," I vowed aloud to the darkness of the night. "With his death my new life as Neferet begins."

When I reentered the gates of the House of Night, Cordelia was, again, awaiting me. As I went to her I began to weep. My mentor opened her arms to me and, with a mother's kindness, she comforted me.

Of course I had to tell my story to the School Council. I explained that, though I can now see it was unwise, that night I had simply wanted Barrett Wheiler to admit that he had done a ghastly thing to his daughter. Instead, he had attacked me. I had only been defending myself.

It was agreed that I should leave Chicago while the local police were bribed and the bank board was silenced. It was a happy coincidence that a House of Night train was leaving the very next night and heading southwest, to the Oklahoma Territory, as they scouted a location for a future House of Night. I would join their party.

And thus I have. At this moment I sit in a lavishly furnished railcar, and complete my journal.

Cordelia tells me that Oklahoma is Native-American land—sacred and rich in ancient traditions as well as earth magic. I have decided that I will bury my journal there, deep in the land, and with it I will bury Emily Wheiler, her past, and her secrets. I will truly begin anew and accept the power and privilege and magick of my Goddess, Nyx.

No one will ever know my secrets for they will be entombed in the land, safely hidden, silent as death. I regret none of my actions and if that curses me, then my final prayer is to let that curse be entombed with this journal, to be imprisoned eternally in sacred ground.

So ends Emily Wheiler's sad story and so begins the magickal life of Neferet—not Queen of Little Egypt . . . *Queen of the Night!*

Dear Readers,

Neferet's Curse was a very difficult, yet ultimately cathartic, book for me to write. While all of my characters in all of my novels are fictional, at times the circumstances they encounter reflect to a degree my own life experience. As an author, the characters in my books come to life, revealing themselves to me as I write. I come to love, understand, and know them in much the same way that you do, chapter by chapter and event by event.

I came to understand the character Emily, who later became Neferet, much deeper in this book. By the end of the novella I felt pity, compassion, and concern for her even though Neferet decided to take the pain of her experience to the dark side. What I would like my readers to take with them from this book is that Neferet's choice is not one that gave her true empowerment. Only healing with the help of experienced professionals and trusted adults and doing the work to regain personal power from damaging experiences can bring true peace and happiness.

If you have concerns about your own experiences or feel uncomfortable about how you are being treated by anyone in your life, turn to an adult you can trust. There are people willing to help you. Your parents, professional counselors, teachers, clergy, or organizations in your community dedicated to protecting young adults from being violated are there to make sure you get the help you deserve, and the support you need to be safe or heal from an experience that has made you feel powerless or violated. If you have to reach out to more than one person, then do so. You deserve all the light that comes from reclaiming your power, and it is a light the world needs.

I wish you the brightest of blessings and love . . . always love . . .

P. C. Cast